Madam President

Also from B Cubed Press

Alternative Truths

More Alternative Truths: Tales from the Resistance

After the Orange: Ruin and Recovery

Alternative Theology

Alternative Apocalypse

Oz is Burning

Stories for the Thoughtful Young

Poems for the Thoughtful Young

Space Force

Alternative War

Alternative Deathiness

Spawn of War and Deathiness

The Protest Diaries

Alternative Holidays

Holiday Leftovers

Madam President

Edited by
Debora Godfrey

Cover Art
and Design
K.G. Anderson

Published by

B Cubed Press
Kiona, WA

Interior Design (e-book) Bob Brown
Interior Design (print) Bob Brown
Cover Design K.G. Anderson
ISBN-978-1-949476-34-7
Electronic ISBN: 978-1-949476-36-1
First Printing 2024
First Electronic Edition 2024

Copyright

Table of Contents

War Zone

David Gerrold

President Bourget was having tuna salad for lunch when the Chief of Staff strode in, followed by two Secret Service men. He looked grim.

"We have a situation," he said.

"Crap," she said, her fork poised in mid-air. She took the bite anyway, wiped her mouth, then pushed herself away from the table. "Let's go." She reached for her cane.

She followed them to the elevator that would take them down to the Situation Room. "Get State," she said. "And the Joint Chiefs, and where's Zimmer?"

"She's on her way. And Intelligence too."

Two guards stood by the door to the Situation Room. They saluted as the President approached. She nodded to them. "Thank you." It wasn't standard protocol, but President Robbie Bourget never ignored anyone. She acknowledged everyone she encountered. The political cartoonists had her shaking hands with dogs, cats, and even the Thanksgiving turkey.

The door whooshed open, revealing the serious-looking men and women in the room. She went directly to the head of the table. "This better be good," she said, carefully taking her seat. "I was having a very nice tuna salad." She handed her cane to an aide. "All right." She looked up at the main display that dominated the far end of the room. The screen showed a regional map, spotted with military and naval resources. She said, "The Mideast, right? What now?"

Admiral Joel Landon, gray-haired and stocky—he moved with an air of methodical competence—gestured to an assistant, who tapped a control. The display now showed a man in a black ski-mask, angrily shouting into the camera. "He's saying 'Death to America,'" the Admiral began.

"I don't need a translator. I recognize that phrase." She looked around the table and added, "The word is death, but the cultural context is different. It's just his way of saying 'Fuck America.' Ignore it. It's just noise. Red meat for the home audience. Okay, now that I've said that, who are they and what do they want?"

Before anyone could answer, the screen flashed to show an image of destruction—orange flames rose high against the darkness of night, illuminating a cloud of thick black smoke and silhouetting an unidentifiable city. Admiral Landon had a headphone held to his right ear. He wasn't the only one listening to the distant voices. Others around the darkened room also had headsets and earpieces. The Admiral said, "Okay, it's confirmed. They hit our embassy in Baghdad."

"Who's the guy in the ski-mask?"

Paul Simpson, the Acting Director of National Intelligence stepped forward and said, "We're working on voice identification now. He claims to be a member of Altahrir AljadidIt means 'New Liberation.' It's a splinter faction of a splinter faction. They've been on our radar for a year or two, but we haven't considered them a serious threat—"

"Until now. You'd better take a long hard look at what you missed and why." The President took a deep breath. She nodded toward Admiral Landon. "Do we have a casualty report yet?"

Admiral Landon answered, "Too soon, Ma'am. I'll have—wait a minute." He bent his head as he listened to something on his headset. "The top two floors are gone. Ground floor is... not good. We don't know if the basement levels survived. It looks like a missile, not a car bomb."

"Where'd they get the missile? Find out. How many people would have been onsite?"

"Let me address that," Simpson said, referring to the tablet he held. "If they had hit us during the day, the casualties would have been our day staff and local civilians applying for travel visas. But we also have diplomatic services and part of our intelligence operation situated in the building as well. But it's past eight, so most of the day staff would have gone home. I have to say, Madam President, the timing is unusual. Terrorists usually want a high death count."

"Go on," she said.

"It's too early to be certain, we're still gathering intel, but it looks like they wanted to minimize casualties while crippling our local operations. That's not terrorism. Not as we know it. This is something else—"

"It's war," said the Secretary of Defense, striding into the room. All eyes turned to him. Even the President. She turned in her chair to look.

Secretary of Defense, Stephen Garinger, was a tall imposing man with an unruly mane of silver hair. "It's asymmetrical war," he said, taking his seat at the table. "Good morning, Madam President. I was briefed on the way over. Here's the thing. The embassy is considered

American soil. So we have to consider this attack as serious as 9/11."

President Bourget said, "I'm not going to consider anything until I have all the information—"

Admiral Landon straightened. He looked grim. "Ma'am? We have a casualty estimate. There was a reception scheduled, there were nighttime meetings as well. There were negotiations in progress. The building was near fully staffed. The death toll could be as high as 300. There would have been top level government officials and leaders of the business communities as well. Our ambassador—"

"Shit," said the President. And after that, a long string of words in Spanish, several in German, and she finally concluded with a simple declaration in French. *"Merde."* She buried her face in her hands for a moment. Seated around the table and lined up against the walls, the occupants of the room waited silently for her to recover her composure.

Finally, she looked up. "Talk to me. What else do we know?"

Acting-Director Simpson spoke up. He'd been listening to his own headset. "It wasn't the New Liberation that hit the embassy. That's a false flag." He waved at the screen. "Whoever that is—" He pointed to the screen where the figure in the ski-mask, was a frozen image, "—he's just a distraction, a small-time player, pretending he's a boss. Here's what we think. The missile was likely a Zhukin-III. The Iranians bought six of them from Russia. They shipped them roundabout through half a dozen ports and ships, passing them through several sets of hands and multiple manifests—they even shipped a few decoys, here and there. They did everything they could to muddy the chain of ownership, but six Zhukins ended up in a warehouse just outside of the Iranian port of Chabahar. We had it under surveillance, both on the ground and high-altitude reconnaissance. Two of the missiles shipped out two weeks ago, but there was a major sandstorm and we lost track of them. We spotted some suspicious activity in the Gulf, but confidence was low. Even with the best of our technology, there are still limits. This missile was most likely launched from a disguised fishing boat. We're checking that now."

The President shook her head in annoyance. "All that expensive technology and a sandstorm...? All right, at least we know what we're dealing with. And maybe who." She looked to Admiral Landon. "How good is your surveillance? Can you find that boat? Can you identify it with confidence? And can you sink it?"

"Yes, Madam President. There isn't a seagull that farts in the Gulf that we don't know about it. And we have drones in the air 24/7. We can find that boat—and we can put it on the ocean floor."

"Thank you. If I ever need to know about seagull farts, I'll call you."

Admiral Landon nodded. "Yes, Ma'am." He beckoned one of his aides and began quietly issuing instructions.

"All right." President Bourget looked around the table, making eye contact with each of the directors, the military heads, and the cabinet members present. "So, is this a consensus—that the real author of the attack on our embassy is Iran?"

Silence.

"Does anyone want to suggest any other bad actors?"

More silence.

Finally, Garinger, the Secretary of Defense, interrupted. "Madam President, we need to respond."

President Bourget leaned back in her chair, waiting. "Sinking a fishing boat isn't enough?"

"No," said Secretary Garinger. "We need something much more definitive."

"What are you suggesting?"

"We have a number of scenarios for just such a situation. The most practical is a naval blockade."

"I'm not in favor of putting any of our big expensive aircraft carriers in range of their planes or missiles. Especially not their missiles."

"We don't have to. We have two carriers within striking range. We can take out their radar first, then their airfields. Then as many of their military bases as necessary."

"How many do you think are necessary?"

"All of them," said the Secretary of Defense.

"Let's table that thought," said the President. She leaned forward again. "I'm not going to ad-lib us into a war." She looked around. "Where's the Secretary of State?"

An aide replied. "Still en route, Ma'am."

"I need her here. I want her input."

"Yes'm."

The President turned to the Director of National Intelligence. "You have that look on your face. Tell me what you're thinking."

"Thank you, Ma'am. I'm thinking about context. If the missile came from Russia, then what was their intention in selling it to Iran? We assumed it was simply for the money. The Russian economy is brittle. But then, the question becomes, what did Iran intend with the missiles? These are not defensive weapons. And... we can't overlook the possibility that we were meant to track these weapons to Iran. In that case, we have to consider that Russia knew what Iran intended. The endgame here is that Russia wants us to attack Iran."

"And that," said the President, "would put us into a major war." She shook her head, then looked around. "Can I get some coffee, please?" She spoke to the aide.

"And see if anyone else needs anything. Let's get some sandwiches down here too. We're going to be a while."

While that was being handled, she looked to the phalanx of aides and deputies behind her. She gestured, "Zimmer?"

Janet Zimmer, a tall dark woman, stepped forward. "Yes, Madam President?"

"On the day I stepped into this job, I gave you a red leather folder and I told you to keep that with you at all times, yes?"

"Yes'm."

"Do you have it with you now?" She held out her hand.

"Yes, Ma'am." Zimmer passed it over.

The President put the folder on the table in front of her. She unfastened the clasp and opened it to a page of handwritten notes. She looked around the table, waiting for silence. She didn't have to wait long. "All right. What was it John F. Kennedy said in October of 1962? Today's the day we earn our salaries." She looked to her notes and turned to the Secretary of Defense. "Secretary Garinger, I'm sure you have all the necessary scenarios, how much would a war with Iran cost?"

"Somewhere between one and three trillion dollars."

"Somewhere between one and three trillion dollars," the President repeated. "Let's assume five trillion—not just because your department always underestimates the cost of the war, but also because we're going to end up paying for all the ancillary damage to our economy as well." She picked up her pen and made a note in her folder.

"I think that's a little high, Madam President."

"Well, yes—but when has anyone brought in a war under budget?" She moved on to the next point on the page in front of her. "And how long would a war in the Mideast last?"

"Based on past experience, somewhere between three and seven years."

Let's say nine, before we could even start talking exit strategy." She added another note. "That means boys and girls who are eleven today will be in uniform before this would be over." She went on to her next note. "How many casualties among our military?"

"You need to understand, Ma'am, we would be using a lot of aerial assaults to soften the target zones. We'd use drones, cruise missiles, and other remote-controlled weapons to avoid putting our own people in harm's way. But eventually, we would have to put boots on the ground. Given a prolonged conflict, we could have as many as 15,000 casualties."

"I see. 25,000, at least." The President wrote that as well."

"And how many civilian casualties?"

"Hard to say, Ma'am."

"Oh, please. We know that the last Gulf war killed 200,000 civilians. Based on that experience, we should assume at least as many civilian casualties in the next Gulf war. Probably more. Collateral damage. What a nice antiseptic term for dead children. I'll say 350,000. How does that sound?" She added that to her previous notes. "No, that's a little low. Let's make it 450,000." She crossed out her first number and wrote in the higher figure. She looked around. "I wish State were here. I'd really like her opinion. I doubt our allies will have the stomach for one more dance in the Mideast."

She started to put her pen down, then stopped herself. "Oh, one more question. What will the climate be like in the next decade? Anyone?"

Admiral Landon spoke first. "Hot. Hotter. And impossible. Might as well rename the equator. Call it the Scorch Zone. 130 degree days will be the norm in some regions."

"So all these predictions we've made about costs and casualties—? They're incomplete. Has anyone factored in the weather?"

"Well, yes—of course," said Secretary Garinger. "The weather is always part of our planning—"

"And just like all your other numbers, you're going to underestimate the severity of the situation." The President put her pen down and closed the folder. "It seems to me that Iran—all the Mideast states—are going to be dealing with some serious challenges. I don't see any compelling reason for putting our own troops in harm's way. The heat alone will be the biggest killer." She looked around the table. "No one in this room is going to be onsite. We'll be sending a generation of young men and women into hell, and the ones who survive it will come back damaged inside and out. No. Just no. We have to find a better way."

Secretary Garinger shook his head unhappily. "Madam President, with all due respect—"

"I hate that phrase," President Bourget interrupted, "because it means no respect at all."

"I apologize. I meant no insult."

"Of course not."

"What I meant to say is that we have to respond—"

"Of course, we must." The President turned around as the door of the Situation Room whooshed open. "Ahh, here's the Secretary of State. We've been waiting for you. Garinger wants to bomb Tehran. What do you think?"

"Bad idea," she said. Secretary Sharon Fetter had served as Ambassador to the United Nations before being promoted to Secretary of State. She brought a no-nonsense attitude to her negotiations, which was why she was respected, but not particularly liked.

Fetter dropped a fat notebook on the table and seated herself to the right of the President. "I've already had phone calls with Britain, France, Canada, Germany—all the usual suspects. Thoughts and prayers and so on. But—" She held up a finger as if to make a point. "They all urge caution. Everyone understands the situation, but they all made the same point. This thing could blow up very fast."

"Did anyone suggest anything useful?"

Secretary Fetter shook her head. "They're still trying to figure out how to look strong without getting any shit on their shoes. They don't want to be the next target."

Admiral Landon interrupted. "Madam President, we've identified the boat that launched the missile. We lucked out. We have satellite photos of the launch. It's heading south at top speed."

"How big a crew?" the President asked.

"Thirty-five, probably."

"Can you sink it before it gets to harbor?"

"Yes, Ma'am."

"Do it."

Landon spoke to his headset. The President turned back to the Secretary of State. "Who's your best back-channel to Iran?"

"Right now? Probably Russia."

"Really?"

Secretary Fetter nodded. "Or we could go through the Swiss. They love this game."

"Go through the Swiss. Pass this message on to the Iranians. If they will deliver to the Hague, for an international war crimes tribunal, the perpetrators behind the attack on our embassy, we can avoid a prolonged and bloody war. That's the stick. The carrot? We'll unfreeze twenty-five billion dollars of their assets in our New York banks. And no patsies. We want the people who authorized the attack."

"What if they refuse?"

"They're not stupid. The president of Iran didn't order the attack. This came from the extremist faction of their government. They want a war with the US. It would give them the political leverage to topple the moderates. This will give the moderates in Iran a chance to get rid of some of their worst enemies. The president will see it as an opportunity. He didn't get to be president by accident."

The Secretary of Defense interrupted. "What about our military response?"

"It's already ordered. We're sinking the ship—" The President looked across the table. "Admiral Landon? How long till confirmation?"

"Sixty seconds. The missile is in the air."

The President turned around in her chair, looking for her Chief of Staff. "Alert the networks. I'll need fifteen minutes tonight. Tell Jimmy I'll need an expression of grief and outrage, sympathy for the families, we'll do everything necessary, etc. Gratitude for our allies who are stepping up to help, of course. Then finish up with the announcement that the ship that launched the missile is at the bottom of the Gulf. The Pentagon will hold a press conference on that tomorrow—" She looked to the head of the Joint Chiefs. "Can you manage that?"

He nodded. "Yes, Madam President."

She turned back to her Chief of Staff. "Oh, and let's put the initial blame on this splinter faction. The ones who think they're taking credit. They're a front, but let's not admit we know that. Just say that we're pursuing everyone else involved in this attack and we expect the Iranian government to cooperate with that effort. Have that on my desk in an hour. If Jimmy can type that fast. Now—"

President Bourget turned to the Secretary of State. "Send a strongly worded note to the Russian President. Be careful how you phrase it, but something to the effect that it would be dangerous for them to sell Zhukin missiles to those most likely to use them. Put it in nice diplomatic language, but make it clear that we are not happy."

Secretary Fetter nodded her agreement. "I'll have the note in front of you in an hour."

Admiral Landon pointed to the screen at the front of the room. The image was a high-definition view of a calm sea. Below, a single vessel was cutting a bright wake across the water. But only for a moment. A streak of something, a bright flash, and then a geyser of water that sent high waves rippling outward—after a moment more, except for a lingering cloud of smoke and a quick pattering of debris, the sea was calm again.

"Don't applaud," said the President, cutting off the immediate reaction. "We just killed thirty-five men. They probably had families. Wives and children. They killed for political purpose. So did we. We are not morally superior. Our hands are just as dirty. But..." She added slowly, "...what we did was necessary. Not for revenge. But to keep them from ever doing it again. And maybe, just maybe, the next people who will think to launch a missile at us will remember this and choose not to. But I wouldn't hold my breath on that either. History proves there is no shortage of idiots and assholes."

Silence returned to the Situation Room.

"All right," said the President. She put her hands on the table. "Here is our official position. We mourn the loss of so many good people. Whatever public statements any of us make, always start with that. Let's focus on the tragedy, not the revenge. Yes, we have sunk the ship that launched the missile. Yes, we blame this group that claims credit. And yes, we promise to bring them to justice or bring justice to them. And yes, in the interests of world peace, we expect the cooperation of the Iranians. But we do not blame the Iranian government. We have no evidence that anyone in the Iranian government was involved. And we certainly will not mention the Russians at all. Nor will we discuss what kind of missile hit our embassy, that's for the forensics experts to determine. We are committed to taking care of the families of those who died. And we'll have—what's the protocol? A week of mourning? Flags at half-mast until the ambassador is buried? Somebody check that out, please. Is there anything I'm missing? Admiral Landon, would you please manage the room? State, you have phone calls to make. Where's my cane?" She levered herself to her feet and headed for the door. "Zimmer, bring the folder."

The President and her entourage made their way back to the Oval Office. Finally, back behind her desk, she sat down in the big leather chair, leaned her cane against the desk and sagged backward.

The California sun shone through the western windows. Bourget looked at her watch. "Are we off the clock?"

Janet Zimmer seated herself next to the desk. She nodded. "We're off the clock."

The President sighed. "Thank you. I have to tell you, that was not fun."

Zimmer said, "It's not supposed to be fun."

"How do you think I did?"

Zimmer said, "That was good. Very presidential. Better than some of the people who've played the game."

"I don't think Defense liked me."

"He's not supposed to. Everyone in government has an agenda. That was his part. But you owned the room, that was the important thing. And you didn't let anyone stampede you into a hasty decision. You weighed the political aspects against the military options. That was impressive. That red folder? Nice."

Robbie Bourget allowed herself a slight smile of satisfaction. "I think that might have been one of my better ideas. I didn't want to get so caught up in the game that I forgot who I wanted to be." She studied the cast member who played her aide. "You're a very good associate. It's hard work, isn't it?"

"Thank you, yes. We have to do a lot of behind-the-scenes preparation. It's different for every player."

"You've been doing this a long time?"

"Not as long as most. We go through a lot of cast members. It's stressful. But none of us will ever share what happens in the simulations. We're sworn to confidentiality."

Bourget nodded. "Yes, I saw that in the non-disclosure agreement. You're not allowed to release any video or evaluations. Only I can. Unfortunately, it's almost become required these days. The electorate wants to see how well a candidate can handle a crisis. I suppose it's a good idea, but I have to admit it's a little unnerving."

Zimmer said, "You should see it from our side. We never know how a candidate is going to react. It can be scary."

"You should try it from this side of the desk," said Bourget. She looked around the flawless simulation of the Oval Office. "I have to admit, it's very convincing. Too convincing."

"Thank you, yes. Backstage is a very complicated operation."

"I can imagine so."

"I assume you know the history. This happened almost by accident. Originally, this was just a standing set, rented out to anybody filming a presidential TV series or a movie. But during the last writer's strike, it became a playground for those who wanted to role-play the presidency, another cool toy for millionaires. Only a hundred thousand a day and you get a taste of the responsibilities of the office. Then during the run-up to the election year, it became a campaign stunt. Now it's a thing. Part of learning how to be a President. So, on our side, we have to take it very seriously."

Bourget nodded. "So, can I ask? What's next? Did we stop the war?"

"Yes, you're allowed to ask," Zimmer said. "But if I tell you, you're not going to sleep well tonight."

"Why not?"

"Because you didn't stop the war. Tomorrow, we go to Round Two and the whole thing blows up."

"Huh? I don't understand."

"It's a no-win situation. You're supposed to fail."

"But I did everything right, didn't I? You said so. I thought—"

"Yes, you did everything right," said Zimmer. "But that's not the point. In here, it's all pretend, so letting you win—that would be too easy. There's nothing at stake. But dealing with failure—that's the real test of any presidency. Tomorrow the simulation gets serious."

"Are you supposed to be telling me this—?"

"Yes. Because being forewarned is also part of the job. If this were a real situation, you'd already be working on failure scenarios. So, today was just the set up. Tomorrow is the real test. What do you do when the best you can do isn't good enough. Tomorrow is about exit strategies."

Zimmer took a breath and stood up. "Madam President, this is the reason we have a non-disclosure policy. Because now that you know what kind of crap you might have to deal with if you get elected—and what failure looks like when your best isn't enough, maybe you'll understand just how hard you have to work to keep these messes from happening in the first place." She offered her hand. "Good luck to you, Ma'am. I'll see you tomorrow morning."

Spooned

Liam Hogan

"What's this?" the captain asked, waggling the offending item in the air.

"A cake fork, sir," his purser replied on behalf of the lowly ensign who had brought the tray and who stood, head bowed and trembling.

"I'm well aware of what it *is*, Hargreaves. I mean, what is it doing on the edge of my saucer?"

"Ah... well there are no teaspoons, sir."

"What the hell do you mean, there are no teaspoons?"

"Exactly what I said, sir. There are no teaspoons left aboard the *Excelsior.*"

Captain Andrews stared long and hard at his purser, a man he had thought he could depend on. "Is this some sort of a *joke*?"

"No, Captain. Not as far as I am aware."

"How many spoons did we leave Earth with?"

"Thirty-eight thousand, two hundred and eighty-seven."

"Thirty-eight thousand!"

"—Two hundred and eighty-seven, yes." The purser shrugged, pre-empting the captain's next question. "Which isn't that many, for a complement of over a hundred thousand crew and colonists."

"I suppose not." It wasn't, the captain thought, something he'd expected to have to think about at all. That was why he had pursers and the likes. "But where are they all now? Has someone been hoarding them?"

"Ah..." The purser turned puce.

"Are you *blushing*, man? What's going on?"

The purser waved the ensign out of the captain's quarters, and never had anyone looked more grateful to leave. Then he firmly shut the cabin door. *Curiouser and curiouser.*

"Sir, alas, I can only give you a partial answer. And I would, if I may be so bold as to offer advice, suggest you forget about it. Make do with cake forks, or dessert spoons, or whatever."

A decent cup of tea was one of the captain's few luxuries. Tea made the proper way, in a pot, served in a proper cup, with a proper saucer. Stirred with a teaspoon, dammit. All that would have been impossible if the Excelsior wasn't pushing itself along at almost Earth gravity, and if he hadn't dedicated almost the entirety of his personal cargo allowance to loose leaf tea. It was a selfish, possibly foolish tradition, and one he might have to give up at some point in the not-so-distant future, even if he rationed himself to just one pot a day. But he wasn't ready to forego the pleasure *yet*, and he wouldn't do so without at least a fight. He glared at the purser, and the purser sighed.

"If you *really* want to know, then..." the man tailed off, wrote something on his memo pad, flashed it before the captain's eyes, then just as quickly wiped the pad clean. "You'll find your answer, and the teaspoons, there. Go alone, Captain, and not in uniform."

Captain Andrews drummed his finger on his desk. The two of them had been going over the latest stock-check of supplies aboard the vast colony ship, one of the first to boldly go beyond the limits of the solar system, heading for a very promising exoplanet. Its cargo was a vast, nameless horde of colonists he tried not to think about any more than he had to. That the ship wouldn't reach its destination in his lifetime was another thing he didn't dwell upon. At some point, a new captain would take his place. One born and who would die on the centuries-long journey, as would his successor, and on down the line until the very last captain of this one-way trip, the one who would step forth onto a new world, and with that step, render himself—or herself, he supposed—redundant. Deep thoughts, for teatime.

The ship address the purser had flashed him was down in colonist territory, a long way from the familiarity of the bridge and his quarters. Deck 14—a part of the *Excelsior* he'd only ever seen empty, while the ship was under construction. A part he'd managed to avoid since.

"Your *professional* opinion is that I don't need to know?" the captain inquired, leaning heavily onto the second word.

"Yes, sir."

He mused on that. If the purser could be trusted, something formerly not in any doubt but, on the evidence of the last five minutes, very suspect indeed, then he was saying it wasn't something that would upset the smooth running of the ship, but would probably upset the captain. Without saying what it was. Very enigmatic, and *very* unsatisfactory.

"Hargreaves, we'll finish this up later. For now, you're dismissed."

"Yes, Captain."

And then the captain was alone. He stirred his tea with the cake fork thoughtfully, and then raised the bone china cup to his lips. Which instantly distorted into a grimace.

The tea was lukewarm by now, dammit.

~~~

Throughout the remainder of the day, the captain found himself second guessing what was going on deep in the bowels of the ship. The truth was he knew, what? about a hundred of his crew well enough to get their names mostly right. The rest were colour coded, at least when they were on duty—purple for engineering, yellow for astro-navigation, green for logistics, silvery-white for medical, and red for security.

But he hardly knew *any* of the colonists. A handful who had come to him to demand favours of one sort or another over the early years, as if he was merely the chauffeur. Then there had been a rare few incidents of unruly behaviour that he had been called upon to pass stern judgement, and which had left him feeling distinctly uncomfortable. He had no qualms discipling his own men, men who had come through the same space academy he had, men who knew what discipline meant. But colonists? Random families who didn't know anything about the smooth running of a spaceship, and whose only real duty was to keep that family going through the many generations it would take, and not *ever* to ask, "Are we there yet?"
~~~

He'd been glad when that trickle of interactions, of both stick and carrot, had dried up. There hadn't been a delegation from below decks for what? A year? Two? Had it really been that long? Yes, he supposed it had.

Almost anything could be happening down there. He'd assumed that if it did, it would be reported to him, by either the crew or the omnipresent AI that connected all the systems together, that advised on matters of efficiency, machine or human. Now he realised he'd fumbled the ball. What if the AI was only focussed on the performance of the recyclers, and not on the mood below? What if his crew never descended to the colonists' decks either? Or if they did, but, like the purser, were keeping something from him?

What if the *Excelsior* was on the brink of mutiny? What if this 'meeting' that had just been arranged for him was the start of a coup?

Go alone, indeed!

At the end of his shift on the bridge, during what should have been his recreational time, he summoned two burly red-shirted crewmen, ex-marines both, and with them descended to the address provided.

Down the corridor on Deck 14 they went, as colonists looked up in surprise and alarm. So many people! So many children—children born since the *Excelsior* had departed. Up the gantry and down into the large hall beyond they marched, into what the AI had identified as a multi-purpose space, optional cargo hold for colony supplies, an overflow sick bay if, God forbid, an epidemic of any kind ever got going, a potential sports arena.

Right now, it contained an impressive crowd of people, colonists all, and all facing the same way. He pushed through them, and *there* it was. Raised on a low dais, gleaming under the ship lights.

A throne of spoons.

A throne of thirty-eight thousand teaspoons, to be precise.

"More comfortable, than knives," mused the tall woman sat on it, into the hush that had descended with his sudden arrival. "But alas, not very much more."

"What on earth...?" he blinked at the apparition. She wore thigh-high boots, in some sort of shiny black material, over fishnet stockings leading to *very* short shorts, (hot pants? His mind suggested, unhelpfully), and then a corset, also in black, with far too many buckles and zips, supporting an impressive bust. Around her neck hung a chain of at least a dozen brightly polished teaspoons. Her face, when he finally got that far, was imperious, framed by very straight, very symmetrical black hair, the blood-red lipstick an almost shocking splash of colour, and she wore—was that a *crown*?

Also made out of teaspoons, the band woven from them like wicker, the points of the crown, six of them, stood erect, each bowl pierced by what looked like a diamond. *Someone* had been busy.

"A tribute, Captain. A pledge. A tithe. You should have seen the fights that broke out as the supply dwindled!" She smiled, waved a languid arm at those present. "All those you see before me brought at least two spoons, some many more. My most *dedicated* followers."

The captain noticed marks on the colonists' bare arms. *Tattoos*. Of spoons. Some of them marched as far as their wrists.

"Who the hell do you think you are?" he blurted, and felt those standing closest to him stiffen.

"*You* may call me Madam President," she said, proffering her hand for him to kiss. He ignored it. A small moue of disappointment flashed across her striking features. "I was wondering when I might receive an official visit. Or an *unofficial* one."

The colonists tittered for some unknown reason and the captain reined in his anger. It wouldn't do for him to take matters into his own hands. No, that was something he could, and should, delegate.

"Carter, Jones!" he gestured to red shirts, "Arrest this woman!"

Neither crewman moved. Fingers remained at the hilts of their riot batons, their square jaws clenched, but they weren't looking at the self-titled Madam President.

They were *looking* at him. And not in a "yes, Captain" sort of way.

"Jones? Carter?" The captain's voice faltered and he hated himself for it.

"You're dismissed, boys," the casual order came from on high.

"Yes, Madam President," the two men intoned, and vanished into the crowd, leaving the captain stranded and alone.

"Now, Captain, there's really no need for any unpleasantness. These people begged me to be their leader, and I have graciously stepped forward and accepted the mantle of responsibility."

"They *elected* you?"

"Well, not quite... but I assure you, that is merely because I would have been uncontested. Isn't that right, everybody?"

"Yes, Madam President!" came the ready and willing chorus.

She rose from her throne—she really was rather tall, especially with those heels—and elegantly descended the dais. "Now, the captain and I are going to my quarters for a little tête-à-tête." Another annoying titter. "Do behave yourselves without us."

"Yes, Madam President!" came the chorus again.

Dazed and bemused, the captain found himself guided to a room off the main hall. It was more spacious than his own quarters, certainly more opulent, and someone had built the largest bed he had ever seen—even back on Earth, where space wasn't quite the premium.

That it was covered in *unmentionable* items didn't help matters any. Thankfully, she led him to a seating area away from it. "That's better," she said, relaxing onto a comfortable looking chaise longue, and tugging at her corset. "You'll have to excuse my theatrics, Captain. My followers demand it, and I *am* rather good at it."

"Why not just call them subjects, and yourself queen, and have done with?" the captain said, in barely disguised disgust.

She didn't take offence. "I would, and it would be more honest, but whether we like it or not, Captain, we still live in the shadow and memory of our Earthly, democratic existence. Hence, Madam President. Future generations, however..." She plucked a morsel from a bowl—a grape? and slipped it past those red, red lips. "One thing you shouldn't assume about me is that I'm stupid. Or that I don't know what I am doing. It's taken hard work to rise from Mistress to Madam. I may have dominated men for a living, back on dear Earth, but have you any idea quite just how much like hard work that can be? I doubt it. And before you assume anything else about me—anything at all, Captain—know that I have a degree in anthropology. Rather better training than *yours* for being Madam President!"

"I'm the captain!" he protested, still standing, but feeling awkward doing so, especially because of the angle it gave him looking down the front of her jutting forward corset. He sat, abruptly, on the arm of the armchair.

"And a very good one, I'm sure." She extended the bowl towards him—it contained strawberries, and grapes, all fresh from the Excelsior's hydroponic gardens, but he waved it away. "Captain, you command this ship. But only those directly involved in its operation, your crew, basically. As for the colonists, you are *not* in command of them. Right now, I am."

"The AI—"

"The AI has allowed me get this far. It must therefore approve, yes? Come, Captain. I am not trying to take anything from you. Indeed, with me as Madam President, have you not noticed how you are no longer called upon for issues of discipline, amongst the colonists, at least?"

The captain blinked. Perilously close to the thoughts he'd had earlier. Something he thought he hadn't noticed, and yet really, he had. One of those things that you don't want to draw attention to in case it stops being true.

"That's because they come to *me* for discipline. Sometimes, often, before they even do anything wrong." She smiled like a cat that has just got the cream, and waved at a wall festooned with whips and paddles and other odd and unidentifiable—to the captain—items.

"You're joking!"

"*Deadly* serious. And not just the colonists, I should point out. A fair proportion of your crew as well."

The captain groaned. The purser. Carter, and Jones. Who else?

"Why teaspoons?" he asked, in semi-desperation.

"You would prefer I'd chosen forks? Or knives?" she appeared amused. "If I had demanded those, it would have impacted life on board rather more significantly. I picked the most frivolous thing we have in any number aboard this spaceship, something I thought it entirely possible to live without."

The captain almost groaned again, before wondering if anyone was listening in and making their own assumptions based on his noises. He could see her point, (the words of the purser, *thirty-eight thousand, two hundred and eighty-seven*, echoed in his mind), but dammit, tea wasn't the same without a teaspoon! He might as well stir it with his finger.

"Anyway, I'm glad you turned up, finally."

"Oh?" He glanced towards the bed, then quickly looked away again. "I'm afraid I won't so easily fall under your spell."

She laughed, a light, musical laugh, one he imagined she must be very proud of having perfected. "You don't have to. Don't you see? When we leave here, all I need do is give the right smile, stand in the right position relative to you, and everyone will assume you are in complete agreement with my status, whether you frown or smile. Down here, I control the narrative, just as I control the colonists. But don't be *glum* about it. None of this would have happened, or been necessary, if you had had anything like my aspirations."

The captain had to admit she was right. If he'd fumbled the ball, he'd done so willingly. More than happy to assume a quiet ship was a happy ship.

Which, from what he had seen, it was.

"Here." She handed him a necklace of silver links from which dangled a teaspoon, a hole drilled through the handle.

"What's this?" he said, suspicious, as he wondered about the waste, and who the silversmith was.

"A mark of my high regard, Captain. Only the most important of my followers get to wear a spoon. Just a glimpse of it will be enough to remind anyone who dares challenge you that you are captain with my permission."

He spluttered at that, felt the heat in his face. She reached out a cool hand, laid it on his arm, and grinned. "Or you *could* just keep it as your own personal piece of cutlery. To stir your tea?"

~~~

The purser smiled, a told-you-so expression on his smug face. Summoned to finish the signing off of the stock-check, but really for other reasons, and both of them knew it.

"You were right about certain aspects," the captain admitted, wryly. "Dead wrong about others."

"Sir?" A small frown of uncertainty appeared. *Good.*

"Are there any other... *developments* I should know about, Hargreaves? Any other unusual social constructs or power dynamics aboard?"

The frown turned thoughtful. "Well sir, there's a guy in sanitation who calls himself the king of the sewer rats?"

The captain grunted. Just what they needed. Sanitation and recycling within a closed ecosystem were vitally important. Someone lording over that could exert a lot of undue influence.

"Better invite him, as well."

"Invite, sir?"

"Yes. Going forward, and for the foreseeable future, whatever developments there are on whatever decks, we'll convene a weekly council between myself and the division heads and Madam President and any others of her ilk. You as well, Hargreaves. Let the various parties
~~~

have their voice, and let *us* explain what is and isn't possible from a ship's point of view, yes?"

Captain Andrews waited until the bemused purser had left again, before he pulled the necklace from under his tunic, unclipped the teaspoon, and stirred his perfect-temperature cup of tea.

So It Began in Every Woman

Darcy Lee

The world was on fire.
And yet, she had never been given permission to act on her vision
All her life facing opposition
Like a cannon shooting without ammunition
She was fearless.

And as her hand signed the legislation
Which would surely get no ovation
She realized why she did so with such elation
She was hopeful.

How far she had come to know such a place
Where woman and man and everyone between the space
Would realize it was time for a new pace
A Madam President in the race
When the one who had been denied, put aside, and almost made bride
Could finally, yes finally, win by a landslide

Madam President

She was resilient.

When those she had already forgiven
Splattered blood with no contrition
Had to ask for _her_ permission
To start competitions, oppositions, and compositions
Which she in turn had never been given recognition
For all the inventions, no one mentions, lest someone start abolitions
She was empathetic.

Because she knew what it was like to be surveyed and displayed by those who knew nothing of her cabaret
She could downplay her display
Since no one saw her worth more than child's play
But she was here to stay
For she could pray her future wouldn't be gray
And fight until V-Day
Was this that day?
She was ready.

The Madam President who advocated and collaborated to bring legislation that would create a haven for those in the basin
She needed no differential equation to see who needed the springs
Lifting herself out of the way of kings
She was ready to show the nation a million better things
No more puppeteers, she was pulling her own strings
When those who tried to cut her wings
Turned her into exactly who she needed to be:
Fearless. Hopeful. Resilient. Empathetic. Ready.

She needed no permission to act on her position
This was her mission
In every woman, a Madam President ready for ignition

The Dead Letter

Patrick Swenson

Fifteen minutes after waking up at the Dead Letter Space Station, Irene Thomson heard the first dead letter come screaming through the Postal Void. She covered her ears while the high-pitched scream pounded her eardrums for nearly a minute. Eyes closed, squeezed tight, she waited for the noise to die down, and when she finally lowered her hands, a single white envelope hung suspended in the force field protecting the station from the Postal Void.

A coup. An uprising. She'd been snatched from her office, neutralized with a quick-acting sedative that one of Assistant Void-President Jax Dodson's cronies—the head of the mailroom—administered even as she fought back against them. They had herded her through the halls of Postal Transfer Headquarters in Ritzville. It was unbelievable. Irene Thomson, five-time Void-President of the Postal Void, had been unceremoniously stripped of her powers and deposited here in this god-forsaken shithole.

Five minutes after the envelope appeared, Jax Dodson came online, his thin face framed in the tiny monitor inset into the interior station wall to the left of the Postal Void. She stood from the bed and glared at him.

"Dodson, you *shit*. What the hell are you thinking?" He didn't answer, only smiled. "This will not stand, Assistant Void-President."

"Good morning, Madam President," he said. "I mean *former* President. You'll address me as Void-President Dodson."

"I'll address you as Void-of-Brains Dodson and feel better."

"How was that first dead letter, Irene? Not too bad?"

It's the most terrible sound I've ever heard. "It was fine. Now tell me what the fuck you want."

"Want?" He shook his head. "There's nothing I want, Irene. Not from you. You're out. You're done. I'm in charge, the newly installed Void-President, and I will announce—very regretfully, mind you—about the untimely accident suffered by Irene Thomson on her recent tour of the Postal Void's Dead Letter Station."

"And just what have I done to deserve this? Was I a shitty leader? Did the Postal Void suffer under my watch? Did the mail not go through? I had no control over the rate hikes. I don't understand why you had to do this. You could've—"

"Done it the old-fashioned way? In a fair election? C'mon, Irene. How many years have I run against you, and how many times have I won? If I was going to be Void-President, it certainly wasn't going to happen unless you retired—and that wouldn't be soon enough for me—or you had an unfortunate accident, and the Assistant Void-President had to nobly step in."

"So you're just going to leave me here to rot? How long can you keep this secret?"

Dodson smiled and leaned back. Irene squinted, trying to make him out on the small screen. "I can keep it under wraps for a while. Until the Void Scream does you in. Have you never heard it in person? See, that's the problem with you, Irene. You've been too distant, and too hands-off. I've been hopping around the galaxy for years for you, touring Void Stations, helping staff and, yes, even coming to that very dead letter station to experience firsthand what the fine men and women of the Void Postal Service go through there. You know almost nothing about how that place works, do you?"

"Of course I do."

"Really. Okay. How many dead letters does that station get in a week?"

Irene shrugged. "Two or three, if I'm not mistaken."

"Four or five."

"So what?"

"You're out of touch. I know the system, I know our employees."

Most of the employees back at the Main Transfer Station thought Jax Dodson was as dry as the arid land the transfer station had been built on: a four-mile square facility near Ritzville, Washington.

"You're a radical, Irene," Dodson continued. "You didn't think I knew you were a Zetti sympathizer? A nutcase believing in that asinine theory of a dead alien race?"

She'd figured he *did* know, but why had it mattered? She was top dog, Madam President, and even though anyone who talked about the legendary Zetti ended up on Dodson's shit list, she had said plenty to him about her beliefs. Dodson wasn't a believer. "They're out there, Dodson."

"They're a fucking myth, Irene. Aliens no one has ever seen? So-called artifacts never verified? *Please*."

Irene was a fledgling member of the Zettiology Institute, and her time in charge of Ritzville helped her conduct secret work for the Zettiologists. They believed the Zetti were real, and someday hoped to prove it. She wasn't a *rabid* believer but had enough of an interest to join the Institute through an Associate membership.

"You're wrong, as usual, Dodson."

"It doesn't matter. You're as good as gone out there, the same as your fabled race of Zetti." He did a mock bow, saluted, and signed off. The monitor went black.

Irene Thomson tried to shake off Dodson's call, and she wished she could rid her brain of the horrible sound of the Void Scream.

It wasn't true, about being out of touch. She could do this job in her sleep if she had to. She stepped to the blue force field surrounding the letter and deactivated it by keying in the Postal Void address, then placed her palm against a florescent panel inset into the hull of the station. The letter fell into the receiving bin below and disappeared.

That was it. The extent of the duties of any dead letter station employee. Granted, they didn't last long out here. The pay was high—more like combat pay—but workers could easily lose their bearings and go ape shit after an extended period listening to the sound of the Postal Void. The job itself was simple: turn off the force field and watch the letters disappear. She didn't even know where the letters ended up, but assumed they were destroyed.

The pay was good for those who could tough it out. Retirement at age thirty. Full medical, dental. Good investment accounts.

But it really wasn't her job. She had to face it: she'd been ousted. Illegally replaced by a moron.

She was by herself in a station no bigger than her bedroom back home in Ritzville. The station orbited around a lifeless, nameless planet somewhere on the edge of the galaxy, thanks to the wonders of the StarZone Byway. Earth had many stations and orbital habitats scattered through the galaxy, again thanks to the Byway, but most of them were hush-hush to all except top military and government personnel. As the Void-President of the Postal Void, she had clearance for some of them.

Four or five letters a week, if lucky. In the meantime, she'd figure out a way to get back to Ritzville and take care of Void-Shithead Dodson.

She returned to her bed in one corner of the small room and sat cross-legged with her back to the wall. From there she could see, in each of the other three corners, a desk, the Postal Void chute, the toilet, sink, and mini-sonic shower. On the metal table next to the sink were personal hygiene items: a toothbrush, toothpaste, soap, deodorant, and a comb. Someone, presumably Edmund Gibbs, the previous worker here, had left behind a straight razor and some dental floss. Graffiti adorned the walls, left over from fifty years ago, when the Station had been a maximum-security holding cell for inmates, a temporary way station before they were shipped off to do time in parts unknown.

Irene stood and walked to the desk, which had nothing on it. Another monitor built into the back of the white plastic hutch lit up, revealing a still image of the new Assistant Void-President Alan Sherman. She sighed. Even the head of the mailroom had been promoted. Void-President Dodson (God, she hated calling him that) had personally set the coup in motion, but Sherman had co-signed the order. Drugged her and hauled her through Ritzville HQ.

Action had heated up at Ritzville, and it was no wonder she was to be announced as tragically lost in the line of duty. Zettiologists had been ramping up messages about Zetti artifacts turning up, and that meant more use of the Postal Void.

The Institute of Zettiology had fought the ban on the study of Zetti origins and history for decades. Ironically, the Postal Void turned out to be the best way to get communiqués between operatives right under the noses of the Mail-Patrol. Most Zettiologists believed the vortex through the space-time continuum might even have been set up by the Zetti species itself. She wasn't sure she believed it.

But imagine if it were true!

Jax Dodson didn't know it, but the last dozen workers at the Dead Letter Station had been Zettiology operatives, stationed there on her signed and sealed recommendations.

Often, a coded letter went astray. A few years earlier, the Institute figured a way to channel those letters to the station. It might be out in the middle of nowhere, but it was secluded and secure. Better to have these letters end up with sympathetic operatives at the station than in the laps of the Mail-Patrol.

Any slips and the whole operation could come tumbling down.

She noticed, under the picture of Assistant Void-President Sherman a link in the lower right corner. She touched it on the screen and instructions replaced Sherman's image.

Send on all dead letters that come through. If a letter is still in the force field and another letter comes through before it's released, the dead letter station will cease to be.

And, consequently, she realized, minus one former Void-President.

The note continued: *Dead letter station personnel's biggest concern is the Void Scream, the worst sound known in the Universe. Employees at the station have specially designed ear plugs. They're stored in Access Panel #3 in the hutch.*

Irene quickly checked Access Panel #3 and found it empty. "Oh, shit," she whispered.

The monitor flickered off, and she leaned back in her chair, a wave of despair washing over her. She checked Access Panel #3 one more time, but it was still empty. She checked Access Panels #1 and #2 and found nothing.

Of *course* there were no plugs.

The Void Scream without plugs. That would not be pretty. She'd always felt guilty assigning fellow Zettiologists here to do the Institute's good work. Frankly, she wasn't sure she believed in the Zetti. They *could* have existed, and she had a *hunch* they did. What harm could it do to research the possibilities?

The dead letter workers she sent here believed in their work, and they had much more passion than she had. And there was something else they'd had that she didn't:

Goddamn special ear plugs.

She stood, stretched, and was about to order up an entertainment vid, when she realized those too, had been purged from the station.

And then the Void screamed again.

It was louder than before. She clamped her hands over her ears and collapsed to her knees as the noise rose and fell, rose and fell, sounding like a zip-shuttle's maneuvering rockets amplified a thousand times, the power and force of the Void itself acting as a galactic sound board. Trying to block out the noise, she rocked back and forth. Maybe it helped a little, maybe not. Her brain pounded; blood pumped furiously in her temples.

Two minutes later the scream stopped, and Irene Thomson fell face down on the floor. She didn't move for another three minutes.

It was not proper procedure to stack up two dead letters in less than an hour, particularly if, as Dodson had said, the Postal Void processed four or five in a *week*.

She was required to key in the Postal Void address and release the dead letter from the force field immediately after its delivery, even though chances were that another letter would not appear again for days. Dodson's plan was obvious, and this second letter only confirmed that he was not playing by the rules. He was indeed going to drive her mad and stick with his tragic story about her demise.

As chance would have it, the letter had come from the Institute. The Zetti postal stamp, a simple red rhino facing the right edge of the letter, also contained a tracking nano that would automatically redirect the letter out of the Dead Letter Station through the Postal Void to the intended recipient.

Get up. Even if she had to drag herself to the force field, she should get that letter dropped into the receiving bin. She thought for one suicidal moment about leaving it there, not caring whether another letter arrived or not. Let the station implode. Take her with it. Let the Mail-Patrol find the letters and shut down the whole Institute.

In the end, however, she struggled to her feet, walked shakily to the force field, and released the letter.

~~~

An hour after that, the third letter came, and the Void Scream made Irene's ears bleed. She barely maintained consciousness. She wanted to reach out, put a foot on the floor, and stop the room from spinning.

For three full minutes the Void Scream bellowed throughout the room. Irene left the letter in its force
~~~

field. On her back, she watched the letter for an hour. She would not endure that ungodly scream one more time. When the next letter arrived, the station would implode, and she would be dead and gone, released from her torment. She thought of her sister and mother only briefly as she came to this decision.

Jax Dodson would get his tragedy.

Tonight, ladies and gentlemen, we pay tribute to a true patriot of the Postal Void, our beloved former Void-President Irene Thomson. Safe journeys, Madame President, and may you deliver your packages on time in Heaven.

But it was not to be. As she looked on in disbelief, the field released the letter. It disappeared down the receiving bin without a sound.

Automatically.

"No," she whispered. She moaned and covered her ears as if the Void Scream itself had started.

"Postmaster awake," the computer voice said from the speaker in the ceiling. "You have a priority transmission from Void-President Jax Dodson."

She wasn't going to give the access code. No way. She didn't want to hear that son of a bitch. Unfortunately, the message wasn't coded.

"Stand-by for transmission," Postmaster said.

The monitor flickered on. Jax Dodson smiled, eyes shining like the Devil's.

"Transmission begins," Postmaster said. "Proceed Void-President."

"Hello, Irene," Dodson said, his thin face split with an ear-to-ear smile. She said nothing.

Dodson, and probably Sherman, had seen to it to stack up special dead letters, knowing she would have no protection against the Void Scream.

"The plugs have been gone from Access Panel #3 for a while now, Irene. The last 'botic crew came in and cleaned up Edmund Gibbs's body, who sadly killed himself with a letter opener conveniently left in Access Panel #2. On you own order—hmm, it *might* have been forged now that I think of it—they reconfigured the force field to an automatic release. You see, Gibbs was like you. He was a Zettiologist, and he was going to blow the whistle on me. I couldn't let him do that."

"Blow the whistle on *you*?"

"He found out about me. About my desire to put you out of the way so I could take over the Postal Void and cleanse it of the secret letters the Zettiologists send."

"Goddamn it, what does it fucking matter what the Zettiologists do!"

Dodson tsked at her. "Please. They gave you a job to do, did they not? You agreed to help them with their Red Rhino letters. Correct?"

"I am curious at best. I barely believe what they believe, but again: why does it fucking *matter*?"

"The station is quite an easy way to handle dissidents, really," he continued, as if he hadn't heard a word she said.

"Dissidents!"

"Since there's no such thing as Zetti, the Institute's misuse of the Postal Void goes beyond illegal. It gets personal, Irene. I'm in charge now, and I must answer for everything that happens to the system. Every unauthorized delivery makes it easier for the government to put their hands in the cookie jar. They might discover other, more serious anomalies with the Postal Void. Other—shall we say—illicit deliveries."

She knew then. She'd always known, really. Dodson had a stake in the Postal Void beyond his salary, his pension, or anything else.

"You're using the Postal Void illegally yourself," she said. "What are you running through there? Which underworld groups have you in their pockets?"

“Our illustrious government doesn’t pay the Void-President shit,” he said. “You of all people know that.”

“This isn’t the way to—”

“Enough,” Dodson said. He paused, then looked at her with an utterly fake sadness in his eyes. “I’m very sorry, Madam President, but a lot of dead letters will be delivered there the next few days. I’m sure you’ll even get a few from your Zettiologist friends, but we’ve already coded a counter-order that redirects the Red Rhino postal stamp to the Main Transfer Station. Figured that out just before Gibbs went over there.”

Irene closed her eyes; she didn’t want to look at Dodson.

“In the long run, the Void Scream itself will kill you. But there are ways around that if you so desire. I couldn’t leave the letter opener, since the Mail-Patrol claimed it as evidence, but I’m sure you’ll find *some*thing useful.”

Irene knew what he meant. The straight razor near the sink.

“As the new Void-President, I’m in charge of seeing that the Postal Void is not misused in any way—”

“Except when you do it.”

“—or does not threaten my own operation. You can understand the importance of this, I’m sure. The Zetti don’t exist, Irene. You may believe otherwise, but you’re dead wrong.”

“Okay,” she said. “Look, it doesn’t matter. I believe you. The Zetti are gone. They never were here. Don’t exist. And I don’t care about your extra-curricular activities. Just let me come home. Don’t do this—”

Dodson smiled one last time, then the monitor cut off.

~~~

The key, Irene Thomson realized, was the force field. She read the instructions on the hull, mumbling to
~~~

herself. "Come on, there has to be something here. Come *on.*"

She searched for an hour. She endured the arrival of another dead letter, barely able to think as she crawled to the Chute and released the letter to the Void. Expanding her search, she examined every nook and cranny, then checked again. Dodson was right: she didn't know much about the station, had never really toured it, but what he didn't know was how much she loved a challenge, and how alive she felt when she tried to solve any puzzle or mystery. She was *exceptional* at it.

Ten minutes later, another dead letter and the horrifying Void Scream buckled her knees and she fell to the floor. Flat on her back, stunned, she waited for her senses to come back to her, and the angle gave her a view of something she never would've noticed: At the bottom of a plastic coupling, on the underside of a plate, near the floor and attached sideways, words were engraved in reverse type and mirrored on a surface that could only be read when she breathed on it with her throat open, as if she were trying to fog up a window. It read: *In case of force field breach, follow instructions at the bottom of this notice to restore full power. This must be done within fifteen minutes from time of breach. Failure to do so will cause the station to be pulled down the Postal Void to its destruction.*

The list of instructions followed, but her heart sank when she realized it was in even smaller type, and there was no way in hell she'd be able to read it without a magnifying glass. Or maybe an electron microscope.

She wondered. If the instructions were there, that meant the Void *could* be breached. Something could *cause* the breach. But what?

Dodson was right. She couldn't survive too many more dead letters arriving at the station. She got to her feet and stumbled wearily to the corner with the sink. She splashed water on her face, then sat down on the top of the toilet lid. The straight razor was on the sink. It could end her torment. She picked up the razor, stepped over to the force field, and sat down on the floor to wait. If it got too bad, she knew what to do.

She did not have to wait long.

A few minutes later, the dead letter arrived. Irene dropped the razor to cover her ears when the Scream rose to a horrid pitch. No sound she'd heard before could compare with this augmented Void Scream. It ripped at her insides, scrambled the synapses in her brain, curdled the blood in her arteries, and tore a strangled cry from her throat.

The Scream would kill her.

The letter hovered in the force field like a holy relic appearing in the sky. She picked up the razor and struggled to her feet. The Void Scream continued, and she screamed back at it while she worked her way to the force field.

Straight razor extended in front of her, Irene Thomson lunged at the Void Chute and plunged the metal blade into the field as if trying to gut it. The field sizzled and popped almost immediately, and a flash of heat burned her hand, causing her to drop the razor in the field. She cried out in surprise just before a concussive blow threw her onto her back once again.

The Scream stopped.

When she looked up, the force field was gone. Only the gaping blackness of the Postal Void itself remained, and within its infinite pathway she heard the whistling of wind.

Irene's head throbbed as she stood and approached the Void.

"Postmaster awake," said the voice from the ceiling. "Warning. Postal Void breach. Force field must be brought back to full power in fifteen minutes, or the station will be pulled into the Void and destroyed. Instructions for force field restoration can be found at the bottom of the instruction plaque. Proceed to make repairs."

Irene sighed and closed her eyes, thinking now about her mom in her tiny condo in Ritzville, Washington, barely squeaking by on her late husband's pension and Social Security. Her sister Aleshia the journalist, employed at the *Spokesman Review* in Spokane for the last six years. Irene wished she had a camera now. She wasn't a pro but bet she could've sent her sister a hell of a snapshot and a great angle on a Zetti story. All the hoopla, the interviews, the accusations. Five minutes of fame wouldn't make much of a difference in the life of Irene Thomson—hell, she'd had years of it as the Void-President of the Postal Void, but who was she kidding? The force field was gone, the instructions unreadable, and she and the station would soon plunge through the Void to Ritzville. It was going to be messy.

She shuffled over to the bed. She collapsed onto it and waited.

~~~

"Warning. Three minutes to bring the force field back to full power," Postmaster said from the ceiling. "Also, you have a priority transmission from Jax—"

"Thomson!" came the voice of Dodson, interrupting the voice in the ceiling.

The monitor had flickered on, she knew, but she ignored it. From the bed, she was out of sight.

"Proceed, Void-President," said the computer.

"What are you doing?" Dodson yelled. "Repair the field! How did you breach it? Son of a *bitch*!"

Oh, hello, Mister President. Are you speaking to me?
~~~

"Irene? I know you can hear me. Repair it, and we'll talk. Work things out."

This is your dissident speaking. Make sure your station is in an upright position. Please make sure to locate the emergency exits. Understand that the closest exit may be behind you.

"I'll come out there personally. I could be there in less than a day through the StarZone. I'll stop the dead letters, I'll cut you in on my—side job. Take care of your family. They've got financial struggles, right? We'll forget all about this. Irene? Irene, are you listening to me?"

She wanted to see him squirm. Dodson wanted her to die, and now he was going to get what he wished. But she was taking the station with her.

"Warning," Postmaster said. "Two minutes to bring the force field back to full power. Station destruction imminent."

Dodson's voice came back calmly. "Okay. Listen to me. The Dead Letter Station is tied in directly to the Main Transfer Station here in Ritzville. You understand? Damnit, Irene, the Void will act like a slingshot. You'll destroy the Main Station. You'll kill *all* of us here!"

"Even better," Irene said.

"Not even you can be that uncaring," Dodson said.

"Dissidents don't care, Jax, baby." Then, to the ceiling, she said, "Postmaster."

"Awake," said the computer. "One minute thirty seconds to bring the force field back to full power."

"How many Institute staff are on duty at the Main Transfer Station on Earth at time of present priority message?" she asked.

"The answer is *one*. Today is Sunday, Pacific time zone. The Main Transfer Station is closed on Sundays. Only you, and now Void-President Dodson, comes in on Sundays."

Irene grinned.

"Irene?" Dodson said, and she heard a nervous quaver in his voice. "You'll ruin everything. Irene? Irene!"

"You'll address me by my true title, Jax Dodson."

"Please," he said. "Please stop this. I *beg* it of you . . . Madam President."

Dodson hated saying that. She heard it in his voice, even without looking at him.

"Postmaster," she said.

"Awake. Priority transmission from Jax Dodson ended. One minute to bring—"

"Cancel further warnings," she ordered.

Postmaster fell silent.

Irene Thomson stepped toward the black maw of the Postal Void, the winds howling softer now, and compared to the Void Scream, it felt almost pleasant. She closed her eyes and took a deep breath.

Just one more dead letter, she thought. That's all she was in the end.

There was no use waiting. She opened her eyes, reached out with her left hand, and the Postal Void grabbed and pulled her in.

The Scream followed her. Or was the scream in front of her? It washed over her in the blackness and lessened. She'd thought she'd die instantly. But instead, she was alive. Thinking. Falling into the blackness.

She landed hard on stone. Cried out as she rolled from her side to her back. The scream wasn't loud now, not at all like on the station, but it seemed to have a presence, as if right there with her.

Then she took a closer look at the stone floor. Zetti symbols adorned the stones in circular patterns and spiraled around and through the cracks and crevices. The walls on either side were pitch black, seamless.

The scream *was* with her. In a large canopy bed that dwarfed the room lay a creature. The creature in the bed screamed in pain. It looked just like some of the Zetti drawings she'd seen on Earth: it was wrinkled from head to toe, as if hundreds of years old; long white hair on its angular head that lay flat, almost plastered, to its skin. It was maybe twice her size.

"Zetti," she whispered.

She had survived the trip through the Void and the Void had taken her to an honest to goodness Zetti artifact. An actual Zetti.

Somehow, Irene had known the truth: the Void Scream was the scream of an alien Zetti. This one, and maybe others of its kind tied into the Void somewhere else. The Postal Void dead letters were killing it. How many Zetti had the Void unknowingly destroyed?

The Zetti stopped screaming, panting heavily upon the monstrous bed. Then it saw her on the floor. It raised itself up to sit, its pylon-like legs tucked up underneath it.

"No more screaming," Irene said.

The Zetti surprised her by swinging its heavy gray legs quickly over the edge of the bed, thumping down onto the stone floor. Irene backed away, afraid the alien might step on her. Instead, it moved past her, mumbling something she couldn't understand.

She turned and saw a map glowing on the smooth, black wall behind her. The Zetti pointed to the map and said something guttural.

Irene stood and looked at the map.

No, not a map. A star chart.

The Zetti wanted to know where she'd come from, she was sure of it.

She could come back to Earth with a real live Zetti and end the feud between the Institute and the Mail-Patrol once and for all.

It didn't take long for her to orient herself to the Zetti map and locate Sol and the planets. She pointed at the map. "Earth," she said.

"Earth?" the alien pronounced carefully.

Irene smiled as she crossed her arms. She nodded deliberately. "Yes. Can you help me get back? Can you introduce yourself to our world? Will you write a letter about your race? I know *just* the place to send it."

Of course, the Zetti did not understand her. Not yet. But Irene was quite certain she could communicate with this alien, given time.

Hopefully, the Zetti had a ship. A way to return to Earth. Maybe they had the equivalent of a camera somewhere. What a price those pictures would bring! Interviews awaited. Wait until her sister heard about *this*.

There'd be a denouncing of Jax Dodson posthumously. Too bad he wouldn't survive the station's journey through the Void to the Main Transfer Station.

She'd be back on top at the Postal Void. Her first order would be to find the resources to build a new HQ at Ritzville. She had a feeling there'd be plenty of capital when collectors laid eyes on her valuable Zetti artifacts.

Most of all, she was quite sure she could finally upgrade her Associate's membership to Full Status at the Institute of Zettiology.

She noticed a copper ring that fizzled when she picked it up. It tickled her palm, then it matched the color of her eyes and spun through her wrist before morphing into a circlet that truly accented the bracelet she already wore there. How high would the bidding go on *this* artifact when she posted it on the Zettiology message boards?

Laughing, she said to the Zetti, "Can I have this?

The Zetti said something completely foreign, but she imagined that he had said, in perfect English, *But of course, Madam President.*

—For Tracy, the original Zettiologist

Enough for Today

Brent Baldwin

The insomnia is back, and Gracie is in bed grading papers when her phone buzzes. She doesn't answer it immediately.

"Answer it." Mikki rolls over, half-asleep.

"I'm not on duty this week," Gracie says.

"When has that ever mattered?"

Point to Mikki. Gracie answers it.

"Got a situation," Seamus says. "Can you help?"

Mikki, now fully awake, hears his question. She rests a hand on Gracie's arm and shakes her head.

"You sure you need me?"

"Yeah. Tell Mikki I'm real sorry. It's a kid."

Gracie mutes her phone and turns to Mikki.

"You've just started sleeping again," Mikki says. "You don't have to do this to yourself."

"To save one life is to save the world. If I had been there for Gini..."

Silence stretches between them. If Mikki protests again, she'll stay home, Gracie decides. She owes her wife that much and more.

Mikki traces a finger along Gracie's arm until their hands clasp. Her face is etched with concern, but also with understanding. She squeezes Gracie's hand. "Be safe."

Gracie closes her eyes and takes a breath to steady herself. She unmutes the phone. "Where should I meet you?"

"I'm almost to you." Seamus ends the call.

~~~

Seamus explains the situation in the aero on the way to the incident. A teenager caught on film robbing a jewelry store and chased into a hotel by the store owner.

"He seem violent?" Gracie asks.

"Not toward others."

Oh. A pit forms in Gracie's stomach. It's Gini, all over again.

They land on the roof and take the elevator down to the bar. Two girls Gracie doesn't know wait outside the doors.

"Where's the owner?" Gracie asks.

"Downstairs," one of the girls says. "Seamus told us to keep him away."

Smart. "The boy?"

The girl points through the doors.

"I'll talk to him," Gracie says. "Stay here where he can see you."

Seamus scoops up a bulletproof vest from the floor behind the volunteers. "You want this, just to be sure?"

She's not a cop—praise the almighty—and going in dressed like one would only make things worse. "No one has shot at me yet."
~~~

She goes up the stairs and finds a dozen empty tables and a darkened bar. The door to the balcony is open.

The boy is fifteen, maybe sixteen. He's on the balcony's ledge, shivering in the midnight breeze and clutching a highball glass in one hand and a pistol in the other.

"What are you drinking?" Gracie asks.

He looks away.

"I'm gonna get myself something, and I want to have what you're having. Whiskey, maybe? Rum?"

"It's ginger ale," he says.

Not the response she expected, but she goes to the bar and finds a glass and a cold can of Canada Dry.

"Can I join you?" she asks.

"No."

She sits two tables away, facing him, and cracks open her ginger ale. The wind puts a chill down her spine, and the soda doesn't help. She takes a sip, anyway.

"Why are you here?" she asks.

"Because I stole some shit."

"What kind of shit?"

"Jewelry."

"For yourself?"

He flinches. "To sell. Mom's a user—was a user, 'til she ran out. She's got the shakes."

Gracie isn't sure what drug causes the shakes, but it doesn't matter. "She hurting?"

He nods. "All the time. I didn't know how else to help her."

"You use, too?" Gracie's voice is quiet, as if she's talking to a scared kitten.

"Hell no. I seen what it does."

That's a relief. Gracie finishes her ginger ale. "What are we going to do now? You want to come talk to the

Community Assistance Volunteers, or should I get another round of ginger ales?"

He shakes his head. "I ain't going to jail."

He must be new to town to think jail is on the table. "How long you been in Hela?"

"'Bout a month."

"We don't do jail here. Not anymore."

He rolls his eyes. "You're some kind of cop, aren't you?"

"Look at me. I couldn't run a mile if my life depended on it."

"I saw those people. They aren't in uniform, but they look like cops."

"The guy, Seamus, is a mailman. I don't know the girls, but they're just scared kids. Lot of those going around, these days."

"I still ain't going to jail." He stands up. For a split second, he wobbles, and Gracie's heart freezes.

"Don't do this," Gracie says. "Your mom needs you."

"She barely knows I exist."

Gracie bites her lip. "My son was about your age when I lost him. No one was there to talk to him off the balcony. Now I'll never talk to him again." She looks away, her tears smeared by the wind. "Don't make your mom suffer."

He steps over the railing. There's nothing between him and a thousand-foot drop.

She has one last gambit. "If you could walk out of here and pretend all this never happened, would you?"

He squints at her.

"That's an option. We can get help for you and your mom."

"The cops aren't just going to let me leave."

"Look over the balcony. You see any cop cars down there?"

He looks.

"We can take an aero out of here. Just us. You can pick where we land."

The wind tugs at the kid's clothes and snakes icy fingers down Gracie's neck. She waits, breath held.

"What about the jewelry?" he asks.

"If you return it, the city won't prosecute you for a first offense."

"That's bull."

She shakes her head. "Putting you in jail for trying to take care of your mom wouldn't help you, her, or the people of Hela."

He hasn't made up his mind, but he's thinking about it. Eventually, he climbs back over the railing.

Gracie's heart dislodges from her throat.

"Can we go?" he asks.

She calls a ride-share to the roof and pays extra for a private cabin. Seamus looks worried as they walk out together, but Gracie shakes her head. He stays put.

The flight is quiet. They land in a darkened park, well south of the river.

The kid climbs out. Gracie climbs out with him, but signals the aero to wait for her.

"You live around here?" Gracie asks.

The kid shrugs, but she knows a "yes" when she sees it.

He pulls a handful of bracelets from a pocket and hands them to Gracie. "So that's it?"

"Only if you want it to be." She takes out a business card with charity names and phone numbers printed on the front. "If you need groceries, rent money, or a utility bill paid, people will help."

There are many ways to save a person's life and very few of them involve rescue from a ledge.

He takes the card and flips it over. There's a phone number scrawled on the back. He looks up at her, his head cocked.

"Things like this happen from time to time," Gracie says, "and it takes someone who's been in your shoes to guide others home. When you're ready to be one of the helpers, call me."

"Are you, like, some kind of hostage negotiator?"

Gracie laughs. "I'm a high school math teacher, so I guess that's kind of the same thing."

"Thank you." And like that, he's gone, loping off into the darkness.

Gracie climbs into the aero and gives it instructions to take her home. The jewelry weighs heavily in her hand, but not as heavily as the boy's life would have weighed on her heart.

Helping him won't bring Gini back, but it's enough. For today.

Darkness Ends

Gustavo Bondoni

Tita Livia Siriana basked in the silence. Her audience, composed of the best and brightest, the great leaders of the great families of both inner and outer Empires, hung on her every word. She'd barely begun to speak, but the little that had leaked of her work, the little she'd allowed to leak, was enough to have them on the edge of their seats. By speaking softly, she guaranteed that only those seated nearest the stage would hear her words, but then again, those seated nearest were the truly important men and women. The rest could get a transcript.

"I am honored to be here, among the leaders of the Empire, honored that you have chosen to travel all the way to Palmyra to hear my presentation," she said. "I only hope that the fruits of my research will meet your expectations."

Once again, Tita cursed her father for his untimely death. He hadn't lived long enough to see the triumph of his family. While his precious sons threw away their advantages and became an administrator in the Australis Province and a merchant, respectively, his daughter, unheeded, unaided and ignored, had not only become Governess of one of the Inner Provinces but was also the Empire's foremost physicist. Her father, of course, had died before her moment of triumph, broken by his sons' failures.

Taking a final, deep breath and looking one last time over the arched skyscrapers of Palmyra Nova off to the east, she launched into her speech. "As you are all aware, the greatness of Rome has spread to all corners of the globe. Our invincible armies sit in a state of boredom as they become less and less relevant. The great expansion that began more than two thousand years ago when this amphitheater was new, seems to have ended."

Those around her stirred. They hadn't come all this way to listen to a political speech. Tita held up a hand.

"I am here to tell you that, in a few months, the great expansion will begin again. New worlds will open for our conquest. And this time, we won't have to complicate matters with rockets and wormholes."

She smiled. Needling the space agency was always an enjoyable pastime. All those well-funded rocket scientists from the Han Provinces, with their promises of glory and their endless string of disasters would become obsolete overnight if she succeeded.

And she would. All she needed was a little help.

~~~

Bassam al Aama was in his element. Nothing in the world was quite as satisfying to him as kneeling over a shallow trench with a brush in his hand and the secrets of an ancient civilization coming to light as he carefully pushed away layers of dirt. Perfection would have required a hot sun beating on his hat, but the powers that were had decided to erect a tent. He wasn't happy
~~~

with the fact that they'd blithely hammered four poles into the ground around a dig, but the main thing bugging him about the tent was that he wasn't working in the open. Archaeology was supposed to be hot and sweaty.

But even this couldn't dampen his enthusiasm. Who could possibly have imagined that, after nearly two hundred years of study, there would be a new discovery here in Palmyra? The Syrian government had immediately sent its best team of archaeologists into the area, had invited teams from France and Italy, and had gotten to work. They were delighted to have the old Roman ruins back in the spotlight. After all, this was Syria's most important tourist attraction.

"Mawal, please come over here," he called.

His assistant, bent over another section of the grid a couple of meters away straightened, stretched to get the stiffness out of her back and walked over. "Have you found something?" Her eyes flashed with excitement.

"I think so. But I'd like your opinion." He moved aside to allow her to climb into the trench beside him and pointed towards a flat grey area, about ten centimeters square, shining in the reflected sunlight.

"Ceramic?" Mawal said.

"It seems to be, but I've never seen Roman glazing that looked like that."

Mawal nodded. "Much too shiny, almost translucent." She knew as well as he did that while glazing had been known to survive intact, the shine they were seeing was extremely unusual.

Mawal kneeled beside him, and they got to work.

~~~

"Why do we need a linguist?" Aulus Fabius, her assistant, seemed puzzled as he viewed the hologram showing their meetings for that day.
~~~

Livia shrugged. "Do you truly believe that these savages speak Latin? We'll need someone who can communicate with them. From what we've seen, the ones in Palmyra don't even use the same alphabet the rest of their world uses." She shuddered. "You don't even want to know the kind of writing that the Han equivalent use. It isn't even real writing with letters—they use pictograms to represent words. Incredibly inefficient."

"How far can we trust him? If he's the one doing the communicating, then he'll have to know exactly what we need the savages to do in order to open the gateway. Do they even have the technology to do what we need them to do?"

"A small electric current through the key? Of course they do. You're being silly, and underestimating them. Some of the tribes even have nuclear weapons. They might not have had the benefit of Roman leadership, but even the densest people would have developed electricity given more than a thousand years! Anyhow, we can't just tell them what we're doing. We need to have someone who understands their language find out more about their culture before we send our message." Taking months to observe the world they were trying to enter before being able to communicate was frustrating, but necessary. The only way the barbarians would be able to stop them is if they refused to activate the key.

He shook his head. "I know. It's just that I don't want to involve anyone else. What if word gets out that we need outside help to open the gateway? Where will we be then? Dishonored and disinherited, that's where."

Livia knew that if it hadn't been for his family connections, A. Fabius would never have been allowed to work on this project. But the Caesar's nephews, even the illegitimate ones, were due a certain respect. Still, it was hard for her to believe that anyone participating in one of the world's greatest scientific discoveries endeavors could be thinking such inane thoughts. It was almost insulting. "If we succeed, it doesn't matter. And if we fail, the linguist will share our disgrace. I don't think there's much risk of his mouth opening inconveniently." Besides, she thought, this man's loyalty is to my family, and where my fortunes run, so do his. But she kept silent on this point—it was never intelligent to let well-connected assistants have too much information.

A chime announced the linguist's arrival.

~~~

Bassam had refused to consider the idea. The single most unusual find ever made in the Palmyra dig would not be turned over to the western archaeologists unless it was done over his dead body. He didn't care about the tourist value, didn't mind the consequences. His team would be the first to study it.

The Minister of Tourism had been angry with the decision, but the Minister of Culture had supported him: a Syrian artifact found by a Syrian team in Syria was to be analyzed locally, if there was anything the foreign teams needed to know, they would be informed. And the defense minister, the one with the true power, had not disagreed—which was better than nothing. For now, the artifact would remain in the dark and dusty halls of the Palmyra Museum, less than a mile from where it had been unearthed.

This meant that they had it to themselves. They'd x-rayed it, weighed it, measured it, scraped it (yet another reason not to let it fall into the hands of overly protective foreigners) and generally studied everything about it over the past few weeks before giving their report to the Minister of Culture.

"We've never seen anything like it," Bassam admitted. In his experience, it was better to get this kind of thing out of the way early, in order to focus on what
~~~

he believed was important. In this case, the central mystery surrounding the artifact.

Excitement shone in the minister's gaze. "Do you mean it's a significant find? Something that might lead to new theories? Or a confirmation of old ones, or whatever it is that you do?" The minister, like most of his peers, was a military man who had very little actual knowledge of archaeology. The only importance a significant find held in his eyes was as a tool to increase his influence at the expense of other ministers.

"Not exactly. What I'm trying to tell you is that we don't recognize the material. It isn't anything we've encountered before in any ancient civilization. If it hadn't been buried in a stratum that dates it at nearly two thousand years old, I'd say it was some kind of high-tech ceramic."

His superior frowned. "High tech in what way? Like it was Greek instead of Roman?"

"It's definitely from the Roman era, since Syria was a province of Rome for two hundred and fifty years which coincided precisely with the age of the soil deposits we found this in." Bassam replied, respectfully ignoring the absolute lack of knowledge involved in the question. "What I meant is that this material looks like it was a ceramic from the heat shield of a space vehicle."

"Have you analyzed it?"

"I'm an archaeologist. I am not an expert on modern materials. I was just guessing about its use based on my impression. I'm probably completely wrong."

"All right. I'll send someone over to help. You'd better be right, because I'm going to have to call in a favor to get your expert." The minister dismissed Bassam with a wave.

~~~

"I find it enormously hard to believe that their world functions as well as it does." Gaius Severus remarked, shaking his head. "While it's obvious that their social
~~~

structure is far from perfect, and their decentralized governments are completely inefficient, I still admire the fact that they seem to be able to function as a planet with so many languages. Some of them aren't even based on Latin!"

"Their world doesn't work all that well. At a glance I'd say they're running three hundred years behind us technology-wise." Tita Livia was bored with this conversation. Since most of the team had had no real work to do while Gaius Severus worked on deciphering the language of the Syrians in the parallel reality, they'd taken to using the gateway as a giant looking-glass into the lives of people whose fate, except for a lucky break over fifteen hundred years ago, could have been their own. Imagine growing up in such a chaotic world, a world in which the rationalizing influence of the Empire simply wasn't present.

"But they should be a thousand years behind — at least! From what I've gathered of their history, they actually went backwards, both socially and technologically for a millennium after the western empire collapsed."

The words "empire collapsed" seemed science fictional, even after months of looking through the portal. Such a thing had been inconceivable even when the Empire consisted of a few hills in central Italy, and had grown more and more impossible as time went on. Tita sighed. "How much longer until we can communicate through the gateway?"

"I've got the language nearly down pat. I need to check a couple of cultural references but, by next week, we should be able to transmit something that is not only intelligible to the other side, but also culturally relevant. I think we'll convince them."

"For all our sakes, I hope you're right."

~~~
~~~

Mawal fumed. She couldn't believe that she'd been summarily expelled from the meeting just because she was a woman. No matter what strides Syrian women had made towards emancipation—and she didn't pretend not to be grateful, since most of the Arab world was much worse—there were still moments when the women were dismissed as fluff.

The most galling part of it was that, though she respected Bassam's experience, neither of them had any doubt as to which of the two would, eventually, become the archaeologist remembered by posterity. She'd already put forth a couple of theories more significant than any he'd ever thought of by himself, explaining the social interaction between lower-class Palmyrans and their Roman and local masters. Theories that, unlike the currently accepted thinking, matched all the evidence and fit with Roman practices in other parts of the Middle East.

Worse yet, the three government ministers locked in with him were probably illiterate. All they knew how to do was drive tanks. Judging by their record in the wars with Israel, and the fact that a portion of Syrian land was still occupied by the enemy, they weren't very good at that, either.

Making it worse was the so-called "materials expert". He'd taken one look at the artifact and proclaimed it "just pottery", but had hung around ever since. He presumably had nothing better to do.

The cleric was the final insult. Even the most moderate among their number felt that women working in professional fields was an aberration. Her khaki field pants would have offended him greatly.

But there was nothing she could do about it. Despite their limitations, all four of the men outranked her. She stormed through the dusty halls back into her office and dropped hard onto her swivel chair. A single touch on her computer's mouse brought the screen back to life.

An image appeared on the screen, the flowing Arabic lettering perfect, as if drawn by Allah himself.

She glared at it. It was this message, which had appeared unexpectedly on the surface of the artifact they'd found, that had led to the emergency meeting being convened, and to her offhand dismissal.

Syrian Brothers, chosen of the prophet Muhammad, we greet you from the world beyond, the Paradise of your forefathers.

It is with great alarm that we have observed the decline of Allah's faithful at the hand of the infidel. With great sadness we see that decadence is creeping, even as we speak, into even the greatest Muslim societies.

We cannot condone what you've done to yourselves since the days in which all eyes turned to the Muslim World for our science and our healing. For it must be said that you have brought it down upon yourselves.

And yet, we cannot bear to watch our descendants become nothing but an irritant, a minor problem, on the world stage. Our destiny is to bring the word of the Prophet to all, tirelessly converting the infidel to the love of Allah.

For this reason, we have been allowed to give you one gift. The block you have found in Palmyra is a gateway, a gateway to Paradise.

But there is a condition. You must prove your worthiness to possess such a gift. You must activate the gateway before the next full moon. If you do so, an army will come to you, an army the likes of which the world has never known. An army that brings back all the glory of the past.

From Palmyra, the entire world shall be conquered, and once more, you will be allowed to bask in the radiance of true godly light. Life, for you, shall be as it was always meant to be.

All you must do to signal your desire to accept our gift is to pass a small electric current of any type, through the message box. We shall understand.

Mawal shook her head. The message made no sense.

She was a good Muslim, if not too devout, and if not particularly enamored of the way Arab society treated women, but she still didn't get it. The message was obviously some kind of joke. An elaborate one, to be certain, but a joke. Which made it no surprise that the men had taken it perfectly seriously.

And yet there was something vaguely sinister about it. Why would Allah, or the spirits of his followers in Paradise, need for the Syrian people to pass an electric current through the artifact? It was ridiculous. If the message were even remotely genuine, wouldn't it be sufficient to declare their willingness in a loud voice? Wouldn't spirits in paradise be able to hear that as well?

She stormed back to the meeting room and burst through the door. "Don't do it," she shouted at the men, who jumped away from their coffee. The cleric spilled a large quantity down the front of his tunic.

Bassam recovered first. The look he gave her was icy. "Mawal, what is the meaning of this?"

She refused to back down. "The artifact. There's something wrong with it. I think it's a trap. Maybe it's a bomb."

One of the men, the one who'd been introduced to her simply as the Defense Minister laughed. "It's not a bomb. I would have recognized it immediately if it were such." He turned to Bassam, and smiled, a condescending, paternal gesture. "Don't be too hard on her, Bassam. She's young." Then his eyes twinkled. "And perhaps frightened of having to abandon her western clothing. Don't worry dear, once the true faith is restored, you will find peace."

"It isn't that! I think something terrible will happen if you do what the message asks. Think a minute–"

"Mawal, that's enough. Please leave us. We have important matters to discuss, and can't spend any more time with your womanly fears." Bassam's expression brooked no argument, and Mawal found herself moving towards the door in spite of herself. In spite of the fact that she knew she was right.

Outside once again, she took a deep breath. And what if she was wrong? What if they were right? What if the army came through the portal on command, and the world was allowed to fall into strict Islamic law? Could she survive in some sultan's harem?

She knew she wouldn't sleep that night.

~~~

On the day, Mawal couldn't help noticing that the government, despite its support, was not running the show. They'd shrewdly let the clerics take center stage. No official communiqué had been made, no invitation to attend. It was obvious that they didn't want to look like idiots if things went wrong or, even worse, if nothing happened, and everyone just stood in the desert trying to avoid each other's embarrassed looks.

Nevertheless, there were plenty of people in attendance, bused in from the surrounding villages, and even from Damascus, a long hot journey away. The imam in charge was one of the old-school types, who glared at the tourists, especially the women in their shorts and t-shirts. He ignored Mawal, though. Her relatively conservative khaki pants and the hat she habitually wore out in the sun seemed to make her the least objectionable female in the crowd who wasn't wearing traditional Muslim dress.
~~~

Flashes, visible even in the midday glare, popped continuously as the imam placed his holy implements on a specially prepared stone, the flattened yellow base of what had once been a Roman column. The greatest ceremony and prayer were reserved for the rectangular artifact, but Mawal was amused to see that the battery—a twelve-volt automobile unit held inside a jeweled green box—and even the cables received similar treatment.

The priest spewed a litany of extremely acid predictions about the ascendancy of Islam and the subjugation of the infidel in every corner of the world while the oblivious tourists smiled and took pictures of him.

Finally, the blessed message, the blessed battery and the blessed cables were ready for action. With agonizing slowness, the Imam placed each item in its assigned position and connected the cables to the battery, one to each pole.

Mawal just wished he would get on with it so that whatever was going to happen would just happen, and she could get back to her dig. She'd been perfectly ready to miss this particular bit of mumbo-jumbo, but Bassam had insisted that, after her outburst at the meeting, it would be much better for her if she went along with the official delegation.

With a final prayer, the cables touched the block.

Nothing much happened. A gust of wind stirred the sand a little further up the road, but that was it.

The imam raised his arms, already in damage-control mode. He wailed a prayer about the unworthiness that kept everyone from receiving Allah's gift. Mawal snorted and was about to turn away—she had better things to do with her life than watch the scene become a circus with each faction blaming the other—but something stopped her. Out of the corner of her eye, she thought she saw movement.

Suddenly, in the middle of the road that led from the west, a massive vehicle appeared. Mawal was no expert on military hardware, but she could tell a tank when she saw one, even though it looked like no tank she'd ever seen before. It had no tracks, no wheels of any sort, and floated, in complete defiance of all natural laws, half a meter above the ground. But there was no mistaking the purpose of the pair of long tubes that protruded from the turret.

The tank moved soundlessly towards them. Behind it, an identical vehicle appeared, and another. Soon there was a column moving towards the crowd, each vehicle seemingly appearing out of thin air.

The tourists backed nervously away, but the imam moved forward, welcoming the wondrous intervention of God's legions. He stood before the tank, arms upraised. The figures on the tank ignored him and kept moving forward. The imam held his ground until, with a sudden whooshing sound, he was sucked below the tank and simply disintegrated into red mist, leaving a gruesome splotch on the dry pavement when the vehicle passed.

Panic broke out. The tourists ran for their buses. Some of the soldiers opened fire with their ubiquitous AK-47s, but nothing happened. No retaliation, no effect, not even the pinging of bullets on metal. The people in the tank acted as if the shots weren't there. The soldiers, seeing this, threw down their weapons and ran.

In moments, the only people remaining were Mawal and a group of government ministers.

"Do you think it's Allah's aid, as promised?" one of them said.

Another snorted. "Were you watching when it ran over the imam? That man had been selected because he was the holiest, most dedicated person in all of Syria. Would Allah have done that to him?"

"Perhaps, even now, he is in Paradise." But the rest of the group ignored him.

"Those markings on the tank. That isn't Arabic," Mawal said. She surprised herself by speaking in this company, but no one seemed to mind. They were too frightened.

"What is it?"

"Latin. It says 'Third Legion of Palmyra'." Even Bassam looked surprised at that, even though he could read Latin as well as she could.

The vehicles came to a stop ten meters in front of them. Someone began barking at them through some kind of speaker system. A woman's voice. Unintelligible gibberish in a high-speed delivery. The words flowed over the uncomprehending group.

And all of a sudden Mawal realized she could understand much of what they were saying. It didn't sound anything like the stiff, formal language she'd learned, and some of the words and grammar were unfamiliar, and she suspected that she was missing most of the technical terms, but it was Latin, and she could understand it.

"We will give you until noon to answer," the woman finished.

A man's voice broke in. "Maybe they don't speak Latin."

"Then they'd better learn. They're going to need it."

"Should we repeat the message?"

A sigh. "All right. People of the former nation-state of Syria. I am Tita Livia Syriana, governess of Palmyra in the true universe and commandant of the Palmyran Legions. We declare that your former nation-state is now part of the glorious Roman Empire. Rejoice at your fortune. Soon, if you submit, you will qualify for citizenship. In order to make the transition as painless as possible, we will allow you to bring us a list of customs you wish to preserve. Otherwise, we will establish Roman law and customs. You have until noon to answer."

Mawal turned towards the confused group of men, mouth already open to tell them what the woman had said. To explain that, if they wanted to save any part of their way of life, they had to make a list immediately. Noon was less than half an hour away.

And then she thought about the customs that would likely be saved, the veiled women, the right of each man to four wives. She thought about the way the woman on the tank spoke. Imperious, commanding. A woman.

She said nothing, and the sun inched its way towards the top of the sky.

One Left Foot at a Time

Craig Kenworthy

I didn't want the job; not after seeing what the prior officeholder went through during COVID. But, as a Zettagian, I was flattered when a group of moms asked me to run for the position as the first female and first extra-terrestrial candidate for the Calabash County, Nebraska, School Board. Flattered and nervous about the political challenges of being perceived as simply the ET candidate.

My daughter, Ritaya, says I shouldn't focus on that. She says, "Selfmom, you don't want votes from bigots anyway."

She's young, my child, and just entering ninth grade. She's an idealist. Whereas, I am fully matured and someone who has learned that, in Earther politics, 2nd place should be called 1st loser. "Earther" is what most Zettagi call humans. Most of them don't call us "aliens" anymore, not after Sigourney Weaver made that nice PSA about it being hurtful.

So, while I refuse to seek the votes of Earthers who hold a bias against me and my fellow Zettagi, remember that, as I told Ritaya, "Honey, it's me or Mr. Botts. It's a binary choice. No matter what species you are."

~~~

It's 4:50 P.M. on October 18th and the one and only candidate debate for School Board starts in ten minutes. My opponent Thurman Botts and I are waiting at our makeshift podiums in the middle school cafeteria (the school auditorium is being renovated to make it workable for those of us who can also hear light waves).

My anticipation scent, once described by an Earther as burning horsehair mixed with roses, isn't stronger than the ever-present stench of industrial cleaner with a hint of scorched tomato prevalent in the cafeteria. I take that as a good sign. Thurman's wearing a dark suit with a blue dress shirt and a gold tie, it matches our high school colors. I've opted for the dark grey jacket and maroon blouse I use when lawyers call me as an expert witness in hydrology. He chose wisely.

Thurman wants to nudge us Zettagi out of the school system by giving parents enough tax credits to start their own charter schools. I've read American history, know what "White Flight" is. So far, we haven't had "Earther Flight" here and I oppose Thurman's attempt to create what I see as a reverse version of it. Still, Botts' "friendly" separation stance gives him a sizable Earther voter base. And, to be fair, a small minority of Zettagi parents are also interested in having their own schools.

The Zettagi parents can vote because Congress offered citizenship to any Zettagi after so many of us, including my oldest brother, died saving Earth from an attack by the Grdsett (a different group of ETs who make Sigourney's Aliens look well-mannered). But five
~~~

years after that, we Zettagi still only make up one-fifth of the electorate in the county. Which is not exactly 50% plus one.

I've decided to do my opening statement in both English and Spanish but not in Zettagian. No, it's not because doing that requires balancing on your left foot the entire time. That stance is a Zettagi thing, seen as non-threatening (because you try attacking anyone from that position). The cold political reality is that being seen as too accommodating of my fellow Zettagi could cost me too big a slice of the Earther vote.

The moderator, a retired elementary principal from a neighboring district, starts off by reminding us of the time limits and the audience of the no applause, please, rule. I keep both feet on the ground as I use my opening to offer data and ruthless logic on why we are all better off together: two species, one school system. Once it's clear that I won't speak in Zettagian, daughter Ritaya teethes the word "coward" at me.

Botts, the owner of the local Toyota dealership, starts his opening with one of his favorite wedge issues, what some jackass pundit labeled "Critical Space Theory." It involves this: right after we Zettagi arrived, some of our scientists started explaining climate change to the Earthers. Based on the way humans were behaving, we assumed that they didn't know what it was or why it was happening. Because if they knew and were still burning all that carbon, well then, *Woyeezittvkstyurtz* which, more politely translated from Zettagian, means "Wow."

Thurman says, "While everyone is entitled to their opinion on controversial topics, it is not the role of schools to teach children things that make them feel bad about themselves or their parents." As he finishes, I see one of the middle school science teachers put a hand to her forehead.

Thurman also throws in one of his slicker arguments: The current system holds Zettagi students back. Take physics. The Earth born teachers can't diagram, let alone explain the 5th dimensional pathway we Zettagi used to get here. It's clear that Mr. Botts is hoping to peel off enough Zettagi parents to deny me any shot at a majority.

Our first question is the one most commonly submitted in advance to the remains of our local newspaper. It's about Advanced Placement classes. Just kidding. It's about sports teams. It's mainly football and basketball the Earther parents are worried about. The golf teams remained all Earther after the Zettagi kids said the only way to make that interesting would be to play naked. On average, we Zettagi are a bit slower than Earthers but are taller and we all have an arm span of at least eight feet. That gives us a big advantage at pass catching or making hoop shots.

Botts answers the athletics question by saying, "Natural but unfair advantages are a real issue. Having distinct schools can help ensure that all kids get a fair shot at making the team." This response draws a bit of "illegal" clapping, but it also leaves me an opening, one I don't relish. But, 50% plus one or 1st loser. I glance at our girls' basketball coach, who is taking up one whole side of a back table, then say, "Always put the best team on the field or the court in any sport. That's why we have more state championships than anybody else in Class C. Let's continue that tradition along with the message it sends to our kids: That what you can do matters more than where you came from."

Now it's time for a direct-from-the-audience question. A second-generation Vietnamese-American woman comes to the center aisle mic. She's wearing a teal sweatshirt bearing the name of our local microchip plant along with three-hundred-dollar jeans. She purses her lips, does a little shake of her head and says,

"I want to talk about safety. I want to be sure that my kids are going to be safe around the aliens."

I ignored the slight and asked the woman to tell me more about her concerns. Turns out it's what I guessed; what happened at Show and Tell last month. I keep nodding as the woman speaks, then say, "I completely understand. I'd be concerned too if my child came home and told me one of their second-grade classmates brought in a handheld nuclear reactor. Thanks to the quick action of our administration, school policies now clearly prohibit bringing any fissionable materials on school grounds. And I still think ongoing dialog with each other is the best way to keep everyone safe." The woman turns to Botts without even acknowledging my response.

Thurman shamelessly generates a flawless look of empathy and concern. He concludes his answer with "Everyone is entitled to feel that their children are safe. And I mean everyone. For example, we now know that fermented foods cause a hallucinogenic effect in young Zettagi. Unfortunately, we also know that middle school human boys find it funny to do things like slipping yogurt in their lunches to see what will happen. Having different cafeterias in different schools would avoid those kinds of risks as well."

Next up is an audience question from the Zettagi. As is our custom, ten of them stand up and ask it in unison. It is: "There so much emphasis on individual competition in academics. Will you consider changing that approach?"

I scan the audience. There are at least three former valedictorians out there. Our high school considers it a point of pride that they hold a more prominent space on its Wall of Fame than the athletes do. Heck, Ritaya is a mathlete.

Translation to Earthers still trying to figure out how to pay for college: "You can still fantasize that your ninth grader will win a full scholarship if you spend enough money on tutors." Translation to everyone: "Most Earther and Zettagi kids are flailing at Icelandic (our sister city high school is just outside of Reykjavik). Let's try something different." As for Botts? This is his entire response: "That won't be a problem If you have charters. You can set it all up as pass-fail if you want." This draws semi-illegal murmurs from some of the Zettagi but no applause.

We're down to the final question, one from the moderator. It's about bias in school discipline as to both Earth-based races and other species. I'm ready for this one. I can cite data that Black students in our district are subjected to discipline at three times the rate of white kids. And I'll say that we need to work to understand the root causes of the children's actions.

Botts ends his response by saying, "Conduct is conduct. If the conduct is the same, the punishment should be the same. We must treat everyone equally." He's using one of the most powerful tools in politics anywhere in the universe: making voters feel better about themselves even when they don't deserve it. Like by offering the simplicity of seeking equality as opposed to the longer, tougher work of fostering equity. A harder job few people might wish for. But I'm not people, right?

It's time for closing statements. I opened first so I'll get the last word here.

Thurman starts his five minutes by stepping out from behind the podium. To my shock, he lifts his right foot before he starts talking, at first only in Zettagian. Yes, he is butchering a few sounds but some of those require two tongues to do exactly right. He's talking about how every parent wants what is best for their children. About how three generations of his family went to school here and the next one will, no matter who wins this election.

At about two minutes in, I can see that Thurman's left leg is starting to vibrate from the strain of being on one foot. I am guessing he knows that putting his right foot down before he finishes would be a major breach of Zettagi etiquette, could harm his appeal to those voters.

My brother died in the fight for Omaha. By our tradition, we Zettagi never say the names of our dead. Instead, we seek ways to honor them by our actions in this world. On this world. And so, just when it looks Thurman Botts will have to put his foot down, I step over and brace all of my 170 pounds against his side, placing my left leg up against the hip of his raised right leg.

Even the moderator smiles as I proceed to then lift up my own right leg. She does not chide the audience when applause breaks out.

Thurman's tailor must be quite good because the man is much heavier than I would have guessed. Still, I manage to stay there the rest of his time, both of us together on one foot. Thurman closes by saying, "I want what's best for everyone and that means letting people decide who their kids go to school with." It's like listening to a more polished version of one of those segregationist Southern state governors from the 1960's. Although their cologne was probably less intense.

I go back over to my podium. My planned five-minute closing contains statistics about how a diverse student body helps prepare kids for the real world, or worlds, out there. It's well-reasoned, even meets the credible evidence standards required of me as an expert witness in court. But after seeing some of the audience fiddle with the ketchup and mustard bottles when I offered too much technical detail in a prior answer, I now know one thing: it's a loser.

I look again at my polished-to-death notes, at all the logical rhetoric. Then I raise my head and smile at my daughter, the idealist. I nod at Zfraw, Kathy, Thwaq, Grace, the mothers, Earther and Zettagi, who asked me to run because they know I believe in all their children, all the children.

I lift my right leg and say that I should have included Zettagian in my opening. That I'd forgotten something important: that respect is not the same thing as favoritism. Then I ask the Earther parents, "When was the last time you saw a Zettagi show disrespect to anyone? Not counting the expected and justified comments regarding the shoes I picked out for tonight."

I make cuts on the fly, saying everything in three languages. I do go after Thurman, noting that while he never uttered the words "separate but equal," you can plagiarize not only words but intent. The last thing I say is this:

"As for the idea of hiding reality from our children, whether that involves climate change or racism? That's not protecting our kids, that's taking away the tools they need to make this a better world for their kids."

~~~

It takes three weeks to conclude the recount fight. It ends after the district court judge tells Thurman's lawyer to contact the elementary school principal: "Because counsel clearly needs to enroll in a first-grade math class. Ms. Mgerta is leading by 36 votes and you are only disputing 14."

I had never told my daughter Ritaya that I didn't want this job. And now I am not going to. Because one of the things I've learned about being a parent, about being a politician? You need to let your kids and your constituents know that you are capable of being wrong.
~~~

But you don't have to tell them about it every time you are.

The Second Term

K.G. Anderson

"We're meeting with Pete and Marietta in 15 minutes," I reminded Gil.

He shrugged and passed me the ball. I jumped and sank the basket.

"Right here, Jason!" he called, loping to half court. Reclaiming the ball, I passed it to Gil.

"Three points," he announced, and effortlessly made his shot. He flashed a quick grin, the one that had melted hearts when we were in high school and charmed voters on the campaign trail. "OK," he said. "Let's go give old Pete the bad news."

Gil headed for the elevator that would take him up to the White House executive residence, two Secret Service falling in behind him. As the lowly press secretary, I headed unaccompanied into the dressing room for White House guests and employees.

~~~
~~~

"I need you to reconsider, Gil." Pete Fosci, the chair of Democratic Party leaned back on the Oval Office couch, shaking his great leonine head. "You're the only one, *the only one*, the party has who can get the votes. We'd risk losing not just the White House, but possibly the Senate, if we had to start from scratch with a new candidate."

Fosci threw up his big hands to fend off any disagreement. "Sure, sure, it's gonna be a tight race. But your ratings are good, you're a known entity, and I think a lot of voters just assume you're in for that second term. Tell me you're in, son."

My boss, President Gil Perrault, sat in a chair opposite Fosci. Tall, slender, with a tanned face often described as "Kennedyesque," he looked like a model for Louis Vuitton. Gil had his elbows on his knees and his hands clasped. He'd bowed his head, not in prayer but in exasperation. My heart went out to him. Gil had loved being the governor of the Southwestern state where the Perrault family had been in politics for generations. He'd never wanted to be the President of the United States.

"Pete, I'm not doing a second term," he said. "Marietta and I agreed—" He nodded to the statuesque Black woman who occupied the chair next to his "—that the vice presidency would be her springboard to the White House. She has every qualification. Far more than I did as a one-term governor."

Vice President Marietta Jones-Petit, a former air force general, national security advisor, and two-term senator from Illinois, had her perfectly glossed lips set in a straight line. She looked every inch the military expert trained to deal with the facts.

"Gil, I hate to say it, but I agree with Pete." She gave a rueful smile. "As much as I want that job, this country is not ready for a woman president. Some of the polls say 'maybe.' But I've looked long and hard at the latest leadership studies. They say that a significant percentage of men will still choose a man—of any race, and any party—rather than see a woman in a leadership position. Hillary Clinton couldn't pick up Obama's voters. The cold, hard facts are that I can't pick up yours. The election would be just too close."

"I disagree." Gil shook his head. "But if you don't want the nomination—" he looked over to me. "Jason, hand me that list, would you."

I passed over the list we'd prepared, and Gil regrouped. "Look," he said. "What about Mendez? Hugely popular governor. He'd do well in Florida and California, maybe even Texas. And Brecheen—he's got great support from the unions and the environmental folks."

Fosci and I exchanged looks. We'd have to let Gil talk himself out. He was still trying to sell Pete on Mendez and Brecheen when his wife, Kate, came into the office. She stopped and stood against the wall, arms crossed. Like Gil, she was model-perfect but her heart-shaped face showed worry.

Now I felt a twinge of nerves. Was Gil sick? Was it Kate, or their little boy, Aiden? Was there something Gil hadn't told us? Some sign that I'd missed?

As his basketball teammate in college and his press secretary since his gubernatorial run, I thought I knew just about everything there was to know about Gil Perrault. His interest in rock climbing (we now had a climbing wall in the White House gym). His love for Broadway shows. His passion for domestic issues, especially education and healthcare.

Now Gil exchanged glances with Kate, gave a soft sigh, and looked over at Fosci. His expression was almost defiant. "Pete," he said, "if I go along with this, I think you're going to regret it. The United States is going to have a woman as president someday. You're denying

Marietta her chance, and you're standing in the way of history."

"I'm sorry, Gil. But I'm willing to be the bad guy to make sure you'll be the good president." Fosci's words were polite, but the tight smile, the confident shooting of his cuffs, showed his relief and triumph. His mission was accomplished. Gil Perrault would run for a second term. Gil Perrault would lead the party to a narrow victory in Congress. The party would have four more years to get its act together.

Fosci stood up and slapped Gil on the shoulder. "You're gonna win, son," he said.

A flinty gleam came into Gil's eyes. "I am," he said. "I'm going to win."

Marietta Jones-Petit, dedicated public servant that she was, signed on for a second run for VP.

~~~

The campaign was bitter. The Republicans and their media friends picked apart every speech Gil and Marietta had ever made, twisting their words and ripping them out of context. They even brought out an old scare tactic that played to the racists, claiming the fix was in: Gil was going to resign as soon as he won and—God forbid!—a *Black woman* would become president.

I'd been worried that Gil didn't have his heart in the race. But to my relief, he threw himself into the campaign. Gil gave some of the best, most passionate speeches of his career. Working with lawyers from the Voting Rights Project, Marietta rallied a network of volunteers to combat voter suppression.

To my personal delight—but my professional concern—Gil and Marietta took far more progressive stands than they had in the first campaign. They carried the flag for abortion rights, parental leave, and universal healthcare. Fosci was texting me during every speech, begging me to have them dial it down, until the
~~~

polls showed the approach was working. In addition to pushing a progressive agenda, Gil was doing what Gil did best: talking with Democrats, Republicans, and Independents, and responding to their concerns.

"I'll be damned," Fosci said to me in late October at a windswept rally in Ohio. "Those two are going to nail it."

I nodded. We were listening to Ekon Petit-Jones, Marietta's husband, give a rousing address to a gathering of veterans. Ekon was getting quite a following of his own. Which was great, because there was something the matter with Kate Perrault. It crossed my mind more than once that the marriage might be on the rocks. In campaign appearances, she came across nervous and vague. The press had noticed. I started to steer her out of the spotlight, using her mostly for photo ops.

As we got closer to Election Day, my job was to preserve appearances and make sure Gil Perrault looked like a winner.

Which, it turned out, he was.

~~~

Gil's inauguration was the victory party the Democrats dreamed of. Their relief at getting another four years to work on infrastructure—of the country, and the party—was palpable. Gil gave a great speech; the parties were exuberant. After the festivities, I took a week of vacation. When I returned, Gil called me into his office.

I passed Marietta in the hallway. Her eyebrows lifted when she saw me. "Something's going on," she said. "Sounds like you're going to hear it first."

Gil's secretary opened the door to the Oval Office and then closed it behind me. Gil was standing at his desk.
~~~

"Have a seat, Jason." His handsome face contorted in a frown. He picked up the desk phone and pressed speed dial. "We're ready," was all he said.

I was expecting Marietta, but when door opened, Kate slipped in. She closed the door soundlessly and met Gil at the sofa. They sat down across from me and looked at each other. But no one said anything. On the other side of the door, I could hear the aides talking.

I went into high alert. What was this about? Divorce? Illness? Wait—it had to be the resignation that Republican asshole had predicted. No wonder Marietta was, quite literally, waiting in the wings. *Shit.* The public reaction was going to be huge. I took a deep breath, and looked at Gil.

"Jason," he said. "As my friend, and as my press person, you're going to be the first one to hear something that's not going to be easy for a lot of folks."

Gil looked at Kate, squeezed her hand, and turned back to me, smiling. To my relief, she was smiling, too. So how bad could this be? Gil was my friend. He was a great president. Whatever this was, I was going to make this work.

I leaned forward, nodding my encouragement.

"I'm coming out as a woman," Gil said. Another look at Kate, who nodded. "I'm going to be who I've known I was all my life. I need you to—"

Kate interrupted. "Gabrielle, let's give Jason a moment."

I confess, I needed it. *Gabrielle?* My first instinct was to argue. Images of tall, lanky Gil Perrault playing basketball flashed through my mind. I knew Gil! He couldn't possibly...

And then I remembered Gil's words to Pete Fosci: *You're standing in the way of history. The United States is going to have a woman as president.*

And so we were.

I took a deep breath. What to say? What words to use? *Gil?* Wrong. *Gabrielle?* I opened my mouth to speak, then closed it. I wasn't ready.

The couple across from me were leaning together, as if for support, and watching me anxiously.

"Madam President," I said. As I spoke those words, a smile warmed my face. "Whatever you need. It's my honor."

An Interview with the Spider Queen

Carter Lappin

Today's Politic Watch sits down this week for an exclusive interview with the Spider Queen herself, only a few days after she publicly announced her intention to compete in the upcoming presidential election. Although the Spider Queen offered to host the interview within her own apartment, our reporter instead met with her in the lobby of the local coffee shop, in deference to the fact that no person who has gone into the Spider Queen's den has ever been heard from again.

The Spider Queen is promptly on time.

"I like you," the Spider Queen tells our reporter, stirring a handful of flies into her macchiato as she sits across the table. "You're smart. You can't say that about too many people these days. When I'm president, that will change. Intelligence will be a priority, not an afterthought."

The coffee shop empties out quickly after the Spider Queen's arrival, leaving only herself, *TPW's* reporter, and a single barista behind. Looking at the Spider Queen, looming in the small space, it isn't difficult to see why some might find the candidate intimidating.

Standing at eight feet tall, wreathed in multiple sets of eyes, hairy legs, and mandibles, this octo-pantsuit-clad candidate gives most people pause upon first sight. Even folded into the coffee shop's chair as she is, she dominates the room, the jewel-encrusted crown which serves as an indicator of her station brushing against the ceiling. However, despite her appearance, the Spider Queen is nothing but professional.

"My campaign is centered around the idea that I would be the best person to rule," she says. "With me as your president, things will finally get done. And that's a guarantee. You can always trust a guarantee from me."

It's a bold claim. When asked about her platform, the Spider Queen shows signs of confusion. The reporter clarifies that the constituents might like to know the Spider Queen's stance on plans for infrastructure improvements, healthcare reform, tax plans, and other political policies.

"My plans are my own. You would do best not to question them," says the Spider Queen. Her expression is thunderous. She finishes her macchiato. The barista is summoned to make another, along with a decaf coffee for *TPW's* reporter.

The Spider Queen noted she would also like it to be known that she is a spider of the people.

"Once I am elected, I will only eat those who truly deserve it," she says on the subject. "Such as people who look very much like giant flies, or those who foolishly walk into webs and are unable to escape. I will also be sure to grant lots of funding to underrepresented neighborhoods and school districts."

Little is known about the Spider Queen's past before her presidential candidacy. The spiders, of course, speak very highly of her, but some are wary to endorse a candidate of whose policies they know so little about. When questioned about the idea that some might put their support behind her rivals instead, the Spider Queen smiles, showing a large set of mandibles.

"I would not worry about the others. I am sure that those who oppose me will see the error of their ways very shortly. The people will soon see that I am the only—that I am the *best*—candidate for the job. I will make a very good president."

The barista returns with the drinks. The Spider Queen passes over a bill and tells the barista to keep the change. *TPW's* reporter is unable to see the denomination, as the bill is covered in a thin layer of spiderweb.

"I am very generous," the Spider Queen tells our reporter, sets of eyes turned downwards humbly.

The Spider Queen has spoken very little to the media until this interview. The public is very curious, as are the chapters of local government and those who have found themselves conscripted into service as the Spider Queen's political campaigners. There are many questions to ask, but the Spider Queen's attention span is short.

TPW's reporter chooses to pose the question that has been on everybody's mind these days: If the Spider Queen is already a queen, then why does she want to be president as well?

The Spider Queen's answer is very succinct. "It is a very good look on the resume, to be president." She does not elaborate when the reporter asks her to.

The barista returns to inform the Spider Queen that her money will not cover the check. The reporter watches as the Spider Queen eats the barista for her insolence. It is an unpleasant process to witness, and *TPW's* reporter would not like to revisit the memory or talk about it any longer.

The Spider Queen finishes the interview with a simple statement. "Vote for me. Vote for me for president. I will win." She then follows up with this: "When you write your article, make me sound good in it. Show the people that I am the one they will vote for."

TPW must vehemently agree with the Spider Queen. Vote for her. She will win. Please, please vote for her. We have families.

You Are President, Madam President

Larry Hodges

With apologies to Lewis Carroll and Father William

"You are president, Madam President," the voter said,
"The first woman to be so elected;
And yet you incessantly think with your head,
As a woman, should that be expected?"

"In the past," Madam President replied to the voter,
"I feared men would resent me my brain;
They believed that no thoughts in my head could occur,
But I know I can think, it's no strain."

"You are president," said the voter, "as I mentioned before,
And we see that you're also a woman;
Yet you passed legislation upon the House floor,
Pray, how do you constantly win?"

Madam President

"In the past," Madam President explained with a wink,
"I found dirt on all my opponents;
When I needed their votes, I threatened to ink
A letter with shocking components."

"You are president," said the voter, "and your voice too high-pitched,
For anyone to take you too serious;
And yet you have Congress completely bewitched,
I find this completely mysterious."

"In the past," Madam President said with a grin,
"I'd debate with a fierce manifesto;
But now I find it much easier to win,
By appealing to the masculine ego."

"You are president," said the voter, "yet it's hard to suppose,
That a woman can lead whatsoever;
And yet, you pass laws that few can oppose,
What makes you so awfully clever?"

"I have answered three questions, that's enough for today,"
Said Madam President with a thundering sigh;
"Your male chauvinism [SMACK!] is on public display,
Which is why I gave you a black eye!"

Upholding Standards and Community Spirit Through Difficult Times

Yvonne Lang

Hilda massaged her temples to try and relieve some of the stress headache that was pounding between her eyeballs. Another explosion sounded in the background and she didn't even flinch. It was unbelievable how normal such things had become.

Whoever knew her term as President of the Homeowners Association would be so eventful? She wasn't going to quit, though. Those sexist assholes hadn't made her step down. The snobby women had gotten under her skin but not defeated her. She had thought she may end up being arrested over the debacle that arose over the flowerbed argument—Malcom should thank his lucky stars she had mustered enough restraint to not castrate him with his own garden shears over his ridiculous complaints. Even though she was President of the Homeowners Association, an organisation Malcom professed to revere as much as Church, he still did not respect her in the role.

Had refused to accept her decision.

Narrow-minded bastard. She had three months left of her term and she would be damned if she would be driven out or let standards drop during her reign.

The alien invasion had put more of a strain on things than she had been expecting.

A rocket launcher went off somewhere in the background, and Hilda gave in and had a quick shot of vodka. She needed something to steady her nerves as she reassessed the latest changes to landscaping rules in the middle of a war zone. The sun would rise soon, and then there would be peace again, albeit briefly. A chance to rearm and prepare as well.

The tenants were looking to her for leadership on how to defend their homes and repel this invasion.

She had not signed up for this, but here was no way in hell she would step down or let the HOA be defeated under her presidency. Despite the swamp dwelling aliens marauding through the neighbourhood, Hilda did not doubt that if they succumbed to the invasion, some dick would point out that hostile aliens had never taken over the area when there was a male president of the HOA, yet they swarmed right in when the first female leader was elected. Logic didn't seem to hold much sway with people consumed with that much bigotry.

The first few rays of morning sun were beginning to peep through the blinds of Hilda's home. The creatures would be retreating soon, dragging a few of the neighbourhood with them for a snack and leaving the injured aliens to burn to death under the Rhode Island sun. Hilda stifled a yawn and went to make some coffee. Whilst the kettle was boiling, she wandered to her bathroom, avoiding looking at the shelf full of disgusting perfume she was accumulating, and began to clean off her makeup. Her skin would have about an hour or so to breathe before she would have to reapply it all again—bare faced women attracted more suspicion than childless women in this area and apparently a war was not a reason to let such standards drop. Malcom had actually made a comment to that affect whilst straightening his tie at one of the recent survival meetings. This was a man who tried to have her time as president terminated early on the grounds she was unfit to lead and may be suffering from mental health issues—because she had wanted more than three pre-approved colours of red, white and purple in her flowerbed. She had added some yellow and orange to give the colours some more pop. Malcom had acted as if she had dug up his late wife's corpse, painted her flamingo pink and erected her as a garden ornament with her display of multicoloured pansies. The only positive thing to come out of the slimy, violent creatures tearing round town so far was he had been killed. The creatures were attracted to water, needing moisture all the time, whether damp grass, or human blood. Malcom had disobeyed the new rules about not watering your lawn to stop attracting the aliens. A parched lawn was just too unsightly to bear and, apparently, he would rather be dead. He had gotten his wish. His entrails had been scattered around his lawn—but the deep, green of the lush grass had looked lovely against his red blood and pink intestines—and there hadn't been more than three colours involved and so Hilda was sure it was how he would have wanted to go.

She had given in to the peer pressure to paint her face constantly, wear nice clothes from certain labels and never have unpainted toes on show. She could not bring herself to smell like the other ladies in the neighbourhood, though. Lynette had concocted her own perfume from some of her flowers and God knows what else, rumour had it some form of alcohol was involved.

Lynette gifted one to every female at Christmas and as a welcome to the neighbourhood gift for any newcomers. Hilda had no idea if the other ladies genuinely liked it, or simply did not want to offend the old matriarch with more money than brain cells, but she couldn't stand it. It made her eyes water and brought her out in a rash. The smell was so common round here, especially when the ladies gathered, that she swore they were becoming acclimatised to it and were heaping more of the putrid stuff on. It would probably be reigniting the disintegration of the ozone layer and picking up where the now banned CFCs left off. Once or twice, Hilda had considered trying to drink it, as it surely could not taste worse than it smelt.

The kettle whistled at her and she pushed some bread into the toaster. These late nights and this ongoing war were keeping her stressed and sleep-deprived. Her wrinkles were becoming so embedded, she'd need a trowel to fill them soon. She poured herself a strong, black coffee (the aliens had abducted all of the cows within two weeks of their arrival, milk was now rarer than diamonds) and started the arduous process of un-booby trapping her house. Thankfully, this was routine now and she didn't have to worry about getting her fingers caught in the familiar tasks of removing the bear traps or burning herself while disarming the flame throwers.

The surviving members of the HOA and any neighbours who wanted to come along would soon be here for the latest meeting regarding new defensive plans. Hilda was also going to stand her ground and suggest now was the time to go on the attack. Defence was only delaying the inevitable at the moment. She already had a reputation as a ball-breaker, may as well embrace it and go after some alien balls.

The toaster dinged as her toast popped up and Hilda slathered it with apricot jam. She needed a sugar hit and after cleaning so much blood and guts up recently—without a hose which she herself had banned as they attracted the deadly vermin—she could no longer face her usual sugar-free strawberry jam. The doorbell rang—one of the dozen pre-approved chimes her predecessor had deemed was in keeping with the neighbourhood—and Hilda quickly tidied away her breakfast, calling out, "it's open and I've disarmed the flamethrower!"

Her neighbours began filing in, impeccably dressed—cufflinks, high heels and all, but their faces showed the strain. Deaths were daily, attacks came every night. The army was doing what it could but was mainly focused in Washington and defending places of interest such as their nuclear bases and reservoirs. There wasn't much help out there for little white picket fence towns with not much else. It was her home, though, and she was going to defend it.

Hilda plastered on a smile and thanked them all for coming as if it were a social event. She passed out coffee cups (all matching—she had discovered to her detriment that mismatched and random mugs caused you to be looked down on) and took a seat at the head of the table. She was so tired her bones ached, but the anger she felt was powering her on. Or maybe it was the shot of vodka followed by coffee. Hilda passed out copies of the current rules they were all following to try and keep the invaders at bay and the residents as safe as possible.

Preserve and hide water—absolutely no watering of gardens, paddling pools, washing the car, bird baths, water features or anything that uses water outside that will attract the aliens.

All metal railings must be fitted with spiked finials to deter, slow down and/or injure the aliens.

Hidden lawn pits must have a minimum of six sharpened stakes at the bottom of a drop. The drop must be a minimum of twelve feet.

All residents are expected to take shifts as voluntary guards for the water supply and act as lookouts for the next attack.

There was also a list of recommended safety measures people could take to secure their homes and garages. Hilda sighed as they reviewed the list they had all agreed to a few weeks ago and asked if anyone had any additional points to raise. There was discussion about whether they should wash blood off the stakes when they caught one, it breached the water rule but was the scent of their own suffering more likely to lure further aliens in? It was a relatively short discussion as no one knew the answer and they were all too tired to talk, let alone argue.

"I'd like to propose we go on the offensive," Hilda suggested. She was met with a wall of blank stares so pushed on. "Defence is all well and good, but we are trying to put a Band-Aid on a wound right now. We need to go on the attack. Otherwise, we are just waiting it out like sitting ducks if we are relying on the government to help us. We need to drive these things away from our homes before we lose any more people."

"You want us to fight?" One mother who permanently wore oversized sunglasses asked in astonishment. If that woman's physical skills were anything as vicious as her gossiping, the aliens wouldn't stand a chance .

"Yes. Not because I want to, but I see no other option." Hilary remained cool and looked directly at the woman. She wasn't sure if she was looking back from behind the oversized sunglasses, but she held what she hoped was her gaze.

“Typical women, resorting to violence. Geoffrey never asked us to go to war in all of his eight years as president of the homeowner’s association,” Jerry delivered this with a sigh as he took his glasses off to polish them on his tie.

Hilda slowly turned her head so as not to upset her precariously styled hair. “Jerry, may I remind you that when I took on this role, you were worried about a woman at the helm as we were too weak and would not be able to run the neighbourhood efficiently. You claimed me and any other woman would be too emotional to manage. So, you are now rather contradicting yourself. Secondly, I must point out, Geoffrey never had to confront an alien invasion. These are unprecedented times. In fact, Geoffrey and his cool head for avoiding a war didn’t do him much good, as that cool head was bitten off by a seven-foot alien.”

Jerry had the decency to blush and turn his eyes down.

“What are you proposing?” Another man asked.

“Nothing too complicated or fanciful, we must be aware of our own limits. These things obviously love water and need moisture. They do not like the sun, heat, warmth. I say we fight them with fire. Dig out our barbecues and fill them with petrol and use fans to blow the flames towards the horrible things.

“Burn them.”

“Fry them to a crisp if they dare to set flipper in our neighbourhood.”

It had taken some time. Hilda had to admit it had been a bold and unexpected proposal, but the residents had warmed to the fire idea. Everyone was tired, everyone was scared. It felt good to be plotting to drive them out and beat them rather than just trying to avoid being killed in their own homes or scattered across their own dry lawns.

It was now evening. The sun had dipped out of sight and the street lights had flickered to life. People were ready, the vulnerable were barricaded inside, and the rest were out with their adapted barbecues and some even had Molotov cocktails, Perrier bottles of course.

The Residents were ready for battle.

Screams and cries could be heard in the distance. The things were coming. Hilda kept her eyes darting around, looking for the looming shadow of one of the slimy aliens, she sniffed the air constantly, maybe smell one first. They always stank of dank, stagnant water. Like they hid in a bog during the day. She smelt the first one approaching before she saw it. She wrinkled her nose; this was worse than Lynette's home-made perfume—which took some doing. She let out a low whistle to let the others know one was nearby. They all turned. She could see the determination in the whites of their eyes. She pointed to the direction of the smell, then lifted a scented candle to light her cocktail. It was easier than matches and brought some class to the guerrilla warfare. The rag caught light and Hilda flung with all her might at the looming shadow. The bottle shattered against the alien's broad chest and erupted. The invader let out a shriek as the flames engulfed it.

This seemed to agitate the others. Some fled and others charged. Her neighbours, emboldened by her direct hit and soon a snaking line of barbecues were alight, like a line of warning beacons from wars of yesteryear.

Shouts and screams filled the air. There were some primal battle cries with her well-to-do neighbours shouting out language Hilda was astounded they knew, along with scream of fear and shrieks from those caught literally in the line of fire. There was a putrid smell of burning in the air, but it didn't smell like normal flesh.

Hilda had a quick whiff of her lavender and rosemary candle before lighting her next cocktail. Then she had a thought. That awful perfume she was stockpiling since it still turned up every Christmas and she refused to wear it, had some alcohol in. They were nice sized bottles for flinging, like ornate grenades. If they burned, she would have a doubly good time throwing them at the invading scum. She shouted out to the person closest to her, simply a silhouette in all the smoke, then ran back inside, dodging her booby traps to get to her bathroom. She swept the entire shelf of perfume into a bag and rushed back outside. She jammed a wick into the top of one of the bottles and looked for a target. A big wet beast lumbered towards her. She lit the perfume bottle with her candle and flung it. The alien didn't just set alight, it was completely engulfed in flames and then exploded.

Everything stilled for a moment after the foundations were shaken by such an explosion.

"Did you do that?" Rose, who ran the local Pilates group, called out.

Hilda's ears had a slight ringing in them, but she heard the question.

"Yes. Lynette's perfume seems to be lethal to them!"

"I'll tell Lynette and she can ring the authorities; we've found something that can take them down! I think I might have a few bottles too!"

Rose took off like a gazelle across the flaming lawns towards Lynette's house, shouting Hilda's discovery to all the neighbours she passed.

Hilda stood; feet firmly planted as adrenaline surged through her. She had just stumbled upon a way to defeat these extra-terrestrials, and found a use for that awful perfume. She readied her next missile. Another alien grunted as it came towards her, some sort of bladed weapon in hand. Its huge feet stomped on her flowerbed. Her precious multicoloured flowerbed that she had almost lost her presidency over, that she had had to fight to keep. Her bright beacons of joy and cheer. Malcom hadn't been able to get her to uproot them and this beast had just trampled them. She had managed to keep them alive during a hosepipe ban, and all that hard work was undone. This bastard was gonna burn. She picked up a flaming perfume bottle in each hand and launched them.

The Bee Queen

Janka Hobbs

I was barely through the door of my apartment when my phone rang. Mama's daily call. I am glad I am close to my mother, but she could give me five more minutes to get home.

Mama wanted to know how my day at work was, who had I sat with at lunch?

I'm almost thirty, and Mama still asks the same questions from junior high.

I hit the "speaker" button and put my phone on the kitchenette table. Maybe I could make myself a cup of tea while Mama geared up to critique my life. I knew better than to interrupt.

"No wonder you're lonely out there in Seattle, Amy. All you do is work. You like to read, maybe you should join that book club."

"Yes, Mama." I glanced out of the window at the apartment parking lot, then closed the blinds. It was getting dark, and I didn't want passers-by looking in at me. I switched on the lights and ran water into the electric kettle.

"Next time I talk to you, I want to hear what you have done to meet people. And none of this online dating nonsense! It's late, and I am going to bed. I love you, Sweetie."

"I love you too, Mama. Sleep well."

I should have told Mama that I'd already gone to a meeting of the book club, and had not enjoyed it. But that was not entirely true. I'd never have picked up the book on my own, but was glad that I did. The ladies were nice enough, and had interesting comments, but they were mostly older than me, some of them had intimidating careers, and they all lived in big houses on the other side of 132nd. The one I'd been to was practically a palace. And the food— fit for a wedding feast. What if I joined and they wanted to meet in my apartment? I'd have to reserve the clubhouse. And how would I afford to feed so many people?

However, attending another meeting was easier than making excuses to Mama.

~~~

So, I went to the next monthly meeting. It was almost a disaster. The book was a vapid romance, and the lady who was supposed to host the meeting forgot to put it on her calendar. We stood around in the cold and made small talk and snide comments about the characters until Mary, who lived nearby, invited us all to continue the meeting at her house.

What a relief! The house was cluttered, and the resident teens were vociferously unhappy about being ousted from the big screen in the living room. These people are human after all!

I told Mama I might be able to become friends with some of these ladies. She wanted to know if I had a plan for that. I needed to find a book to suggest for a future meeting.
~~~

~~~

Maybe it was just that I was paying attention, maybe I'd googled one too many book reviews, but my computer was suddenly full of book recommendations. They were not all for the same book—that would have been creepy—but a lot of them were for a book called *Be a Queen Bee*, by Martine Abel. Reviews were mostly four and five stars, probably not all fake. I could not find much about the author, but lots of writers used pseudonyms. Also, the publisher was putting on some contests for readers that might be fun to try with the group.

I stopped by a bookstore and bought a copy. The cover was a watercolory picture of a woman in a yellow suit, with bee's wings, who looked remarkably like the author picture on the back. The endnotes contained lots of links to the contest website, and not much else.

I took a cup of tea to bed and started reading. The book talked about how queen bees are treated differently from worker bees from larva-hood. It contrasted that with the way children are brought up among different classes of people, and the different expectations placed on them.

The first section concluded with a recipe for "modified royal jelly," what bees feed their larvae to make them grow up to be queens, plus vitamins especially for humans.

On a whim, I sent away for the fancy ingredients and made the recipe. It was tasty in a candyish sort of way, and I took some of the jelly to work for a treat the next day. To my surprise, I not only stayed awake in the afternoon staff meeting, I even spoke up when Matt suggested that women in the office should be asked to wear skirts. I surprised myself by telling him to quit being sexist. He fake apologized, and said it was a joke. Not much of a win, but better than just sitting there.
~~~

~~~

At the next month's book club meeting, I asked if anyone knew about the queen bee book. Petra said she'd heard it got good reviews.

Laurie looked it up on her phone. "Oh, look! They're having a contest for book clubs. Whichever 'hive' gathers the most 'honey' gets to pick one of their members as 'queen bee'. There's all sorts of prizes. Including a weeklong cruise for five members of the club."

I'd never been on a cruise before. It might be fun.

"Only five?" Nona frowned. "There are more than twelve of us here."

"Maybe they'll let us pay for extras," Sheilagh said. "Otherwise, I guess we will draw straws."

"We need to try this!" said Mary. "Amy, it was your idea, why don't you organize it?"

Me? My first thought, of course, was "I can't!" then I barely stopped myself from blurting "Who are you to boss me around?" I had to watch out for what I was beginning to call "royal jelly thoughts!"

Before I could formulate a more polite way to say it, I remembered a passage later in the book. "Human society is more complex than a honeybee hive, and a human queen bee needs to look beyond the immediate situation, to an ultimate goal." If I wanted these ladies to be my friends, I should play along. If they all wanted to go on a cruise, I'd do my best to win it for them. How hard could it be?

"Should we read this for our next book?" I asked instead.

"Yes!" Mary gushed.

I looked around at the circle of women. "Everyone who wants to read Bee Queen for our next book, raise your hand."

Most of the hands went up, and after a moment, the rest followed.
~~~

"Amy, tell us when the next meeting is," Mary said.

This was moving way too fast. They wanted me to tell them what day we were meeting?

"I'll have to see if I can reserve the clubhouse; my apartment isn't big enough for everybody."

"If you can't get the clubhouse, we can meet at my house instead," said Sheilagh. "And I nominate Amy for Club President. We need someone to keep us organized!"

"I second that!" Laurie added.

Before I could decide whether my response was "well, um, okay" or "no way, not me!", the book club voted (unanimously again) and were congratulating me and clapping me on the back. I wondered if Mama would be happy about this, or if I would just get a lecture about "those rich women making you do all the work." I needed to get over worrying about what Mama would say. I'd never been elected to anything before. It was kind of exciting.

As the new Book Club President, I got right to work filling out the entry form for the contest. We didn't need to read the book to start on that.

The first challenge from the website was to gather "at least one ton" of food for the local food bank. A couple of weekends in front of the grocery store, and participation of member's' kids (teenagers who needed community service for school), and that was done; I carefully tallied the weights of all the items, and Mary called a local TV station to have a reporter there when the truck came to pick up the food. We had nearly two tons, and a heartwarming story with prominent mention of the Queen Bee contest.

For the second challenge, the publisher sent me a set of questions about the "leadership qualities" of each of the other book club members. I took a sip of Royal Jelly, and pictured each member of the club. It felt a bit weird, but at least I'd gotten to know most of them better during our food bank project.

When I sent in my answers, I was issued a password to a hidden part of the "Queen Bee Contest" website, with a list of challenges to accomplish using club member's strengths, and a reminder that "the Queen Bee accomplishes these challenges for the good of the hive!" The challenges included "asks," requests to other members to do tasks for me—simple things that illustrated their capabilities.

I also clicked on the ad for "Bee Queen Pheromone Scent," and ordered a sample bottle. It arrived the next day. It smelled a bit earthy, but when I sprayed it on my wrist and sniffed it, I felt calm and in control.

I asked Laurie to help me with a project for work. I cajoled Nona into helping me make pastries for Mama's birthday. Megan gave me a horseback riding lesson, which was fun, if a bit scary. I logged the completed challenges into the website, and watched our points add up.

For a bonus challenge, I sent out an email to the group with a coupon code for Royal Jelly ingredients. All part of the game, right? Also, all for the good of the hive! I was almost surprised when "you have ordering points!" showed up on my account.

I put in yet another order for Royal Jelly ingredients. I was going through enough that, even with limited shelf life, it would be cheaper to order in bulk. The next day, a "Bee Queen Affirmation" arrived in my in-box. From then on, every morning, a new affirmation arrived: "What is good for the Queen is good for the Hive!" "Where the Queen leads, the Hive follows!"

The next Hive challenge was to get the whole club together to answer questions about the book for a video quiz with the publisher. This one worried me a little. What if not everybody had read the book? I sent out an e-mail to schedule an extra meeting for the quiz after we met to discuss the book among ourselves. Also, did anyone have a good computer set up for the video quiz? No one complained. I was becoming a Bee Queen and leading my hive!

At least I'd enjoyed most of the book. The ending was a bit weird, talking about some "genetics of leadership" stuff that didn't quite make sense. Maybe one of the other ladies would explain it during the meeting. I was having fun with the contest planning, though, and that was good enough.

Also, my new, assertive Queen Bee personality seemed to be a hit at work. Grant asked me to take on new projects, and even hinted at a raise.

I filled out the reservation form for the apartment clubhouse, thinking about everything I'd need to prepare. So much to do! Instead of hitting "send," I called Sheilagh. "Is your offer to host the next book club meeting still valid? I'm swamped at work right now! I promise to host some other time!"

"That's all right. I enjoy having people here, and I'm used to cooking for a large family. Just come on over. We'll ace that quiz. I look forward to that cruise."

"Thanks!" I hung up, equally grateful and thrilled that another ask had worked successfully.

The big day arrived. I drove to Sheilagh's, wearing my new perfume, with a plate of cookies and two bottles of diet Pepsi (Sheilagh's favorite), along with my annotated copy of the book, and a list of "questions for book clubs" from the publisher. I'd spent an hour picking out an outfit that looked relaxed and casual, and, oddly, reminded me of the author photo at the back of the book.

Mary came in right behind me. "This is going to be fun! I love quiz shows!"

"What part of the book did you like best?" I asked her.

"The part about the bees!"

I suppressed an eye roll. "You, um, you did read the book?"

Mary smiled and went to the counter to pour herself a glass of wine.

So, Mary had not read the book. Was that part of my challenge? Had everyone in the book club been given a challenge? Or a secret assignment? That would make so much sense!

The rest of the ladies arrived and gathered around the island in Sheilagh's kitchen, sipping and snacking, updating each other on kids/jobs/spouses/other neighbors. I listened to them buzz, waiting for the right moment to dance them into the living room to begin the meeting. Sheilagh was still bustling about, but it was her house, so maybe that was her prerogative?

The doorbell rang. Sheilagh answered the door, and welcomed an unfamiliar blonde woman into the house. She was wearing pumps, a well tailored black skirt, and a gold suit jacket with black trim. I recognized her from somewhere. Had she come to book club before?

Sheilagh led the woman into the kitchen, a huge grin on her face. "Ladies, I would like you to meet Martine."

Martine? As in Martine Abel? As in, OMG, the author of the book? Had Sheilagh invited Martine? Was Martine going to do the quiz in person?

Conversation stopped. I set my glass down harder than I intended, and my wine sloshed on the counter. I reached for a napkin to mop it up.

Of course, by then Martine was surrounded, with everyone asking questions and saying nice things about the book. It was interesting to see who was talking and who was hanging back. Maybe I was okay with hanging back?

Sheilagh presented Martine with a glass of wine and a plate of snacks, and announced "Maybe we should move to the living room to talk."

I stepped forward to introduce myself. Martine looked straight at me, and flashed a million dollar smile. "You must be Amy. So glad to finally meet you. Such a promising Queen Bee."

I made myself smile back. I had been looking forward to hearing what the ladies really thought of the book, but with the author present, they would all be on their best behavior. Also, it would not be the relaxed evening I'd been hoping for. Oh, well, 'a Queen Bee is always ready to act for her hive.' "We are honored by your presence. What a surprise!" I gestured Martine toward the living room. "After you!"

When we were all seated, Martine graced us with another smile, and asked, "so what did you think?"

Mary gushed enthusiastically over the descriptions of the bee dances (That was from the back cover blurb). Laurie (our analytic) asked questions about hive social structure. I kept track of who had already spoken, and made sure everyone got a chance to talk. I also kept a close eye on Martine's expressions, and stepped in gently a couple of times to steer the conversation. It was easy to tell when someone said something Martine did not like. The corner of her eye twitched, though her smile never wavered.

When Sheilagh stepped out to the kitchen to refill her glass, I followed her. "How did you get Martine to come?"

Sheilagh laughed. "I thought you asked her! I got an e-mail from the contest people, wanting to know our meeting calendar, so they could schedule the video interviews. When I answered, I got the response "Martine has accepted your invitation!"

I remembered to close my mouth. “Wow. That is some level of confidence!”

Sheilagh laughed again. “It is. We’d better get back out there, to see how our chances are going.”

I returned to the living room in time to catch Martine’s response to what was probably a question from Laurie. “Of course there are differences between humans and bees! Humans are much more complex! However, bees are a very good metaphor for human society, and can help us examine ourselves at a comprehensible scale.”

“How does your assertion that becoming a queen bee is all in the upbringing tie in with the discussion of genetics at the end of the book?” I blurted out the question without considering how it would impact the conversation.

Martine glared at me for a microsecond before the ubiquitous smile returned. “As I just said, humans are more complex than bees. Obviously, not everyone can be a Queen Bee. Not every hive will prosper.” I barely stopped myself from cringing. Had I just destroyed the club’s chances with a simple question?

Martine tossed her head. “If a queen bee’s genetics are inferior, the hive fails. In human society, somebody else steps in to lead. It’s really not that different.”

What else was there to say? Maybe I should let Martine end the meeting? But what kind of leadership would that be? I waited for another lull, and stood up. “We should all thank Martine for coming to our meeting. What an honor! I am sure we have kept her late enough.”

Martine shot me a glance that I could not decipher. Had I screwed up again? But the bland smile was back. I couldn’t do anything about it now. The whole crew walked Martine to the door. As she was leaving, Martine asked me, “I presume you come from a long line of leaders?”

I thought for a moment. Mama played first violin in the community orchestra. Grandma ran the craft division at the county fair. Great-gran had organized a soup kitchen during the depression. "Of course!" I said.

~~~

On my way home, I thought about Martine's last comment, and my own response. My family had never been rich, or political, or any of the big things people usually associated with leadership. But they did each take charge in their own small ways. Except for me. I had never led anything, before now. And, well, maybe this had been my chance. And I was sure I had blown it.

I needn't have worried. A few days later, an invitation arrived from the Bee Queen publisher to come to New York for the final round. Unfortunately, it did not come with a plane ticket, and my raise had not been that big. I called Mary to complain. Mary offered to pay for the ticket, and the fancy hotel where the final round was being held. Super nice that at least she still believed in me! I documented her gift, and sent it in as a bonus hive challenge, just in case they were still scoring those.

~~~

I did my best to look professional, spritzed myself with Queen Bee Perfume, and had a sip of Royal Jelly before heading down to the hotel restaurant for breakfast. Despite being nervous, I needed to keep my strength up. Also, it was a good place to watch the competition.

The hotel was full of book club looking women, mostly milling about. How many finalists were there?

I got to the conference room early. Long tables, covered with alternating yellow and black tablecloths, vases of flowers in the middle, a glass of water at each place. The room already smelled of Queen Bee pheromone perfume. I found a seat near the stage, with a good view of the podium.

At exactly 9:00, a blonde lady in a suit very similar to the one Martine had worn stepped up to the podium and introduced herself as Audra. "Welcome, aspiring Queen Bees!"

I cheered along with the rest of the room.

"Are you ready to prove yourself Queen?"

Another cheer.

"For this round, you will each be sent a list of phone numbers of book club members, not people from your own club. You have their name, the club's Queen Bee's description of the person, and a list of actions. You need to convince that person to do something on the list. You will see that more difficult asks will award more points.

"I hope your phones are charged. We will go till lunch time. When the timer rings, hang up and put down your phone."

That was a new twist on the contest, but was it really so different from the other challenges? My phone dinged as the list arrived. Most of the tasks had to do with money, some were just silly, and a few sounded really embarrassing. I decided to start with money. It was the most straightforward. I warmed up by convincing a couple of the ladies on my list to order Royal Jelly in bulk. "It will bring our book club more points!" was effective, even though we were not in the same club. Then, I tackled a big one – convincing someone to send money for a plane ticket, just as Mary had done for me. The argument "Your Queen Bee lost her purse" actually worked! I talked a couple of people into ordering pheromone perfume for their entire club, and was just about to go after one of the silly asks when the timer rang.

As we filed out for lunch, I noticed Audra handing out slips of paper. None of the ladies getting the slips looked happy. One glanced at her paper and burst into tears. They were being asked to leave. I felt butterflies as Audra simply smiled when I filed past.

An hour to grab lunch, then back to the conference room. More of the same, albeit with fewer people. It was exhausting, but Martine herself stopped by twice to encourage me, which made me even more determined to win.

At the end of the day, there was a nice dinner in the hotel restaurant, and, when Audra handed out envelopes to a few of us, I discovered that I had been moved to a deluxe room. There was even a sign on the door that said "Queen Bee."

I called Mary, who had bought a case of Royal Jelly, thinking it was for our club, and Sheilagh, who had filmed herself dancing in a silly costume. I assured them they'd helped, even though I knew they had been tricked into supporting a different hive. I didn't want to make them sad.

The next day, we were all given a different list of challenges, and a new list of numbers.

Some of these were asks for increasingly large amounts of money, and some were really embarrassing. I even had a few failures, the worst of which was when I attempted one of the embarrassing asks, and the woman actually broke down in tears.

I set down my phone and took a deep breath and a drink of water before going on to gather more orders for jumbo bottles of pheromone perfume. At least those would not make anybody cry.

Martine stopped by a few minutes later. "You looked unhappy a few minutes ago. What happened?"

I looked up into her face, trying to read it. "I made someone cry. I don't like making people cry."

That smile again. "If she's not up to playing, she doesn't have to play. Don't let it bother you." She put a hand on my shoulder. "You are one of our most promising Queen Bees. One more day of tests, and you will win the cruise."

"For me and my book club?" I asked.

"Oh, the cruise is for the queen, they are just worker bees."

"But I would never have gotten here without them!"

Martine gave a shallow smile. "They will be pleased to see you succeed."

"The contest rules said 'five members of the club'."

"We had to change that. This venue is pricey." That fake smile again. "But I know they'll be proud of you. They really will!" She patted my shoulder and flounced off to speak to another hopeful. As if what she was doing was perfectly acceptable. I took a deep sniff of my perfume, hoping to calm the buzzing in my ears. It did not help.

That evening, I stopped at the hotel gift store and bought a fat black pen. When I got back to the deluxe room, I crossed out "Queen Bee", and wrote in "Book Club President."

I brushed my hair, spritzed on some Queen Bee pheromone perfume, took a sip of Royal Jelly, and sat down on the bed. I called Mama, just because I always talked to Mama (Yes, Mama, it is a nice hotel, everything is very clean). A few minutes later, someone knocked on the door.

"Amy? It's Audra!"

"Just a minute!" I took a deep breath and counted to twenty before opening the door.

Audra was frowning. "Someone defaced your Queen Bee sign."

"Martine said that you're only sending Queen Bees on the cruise?"

Audra's expression changed back to a fake smile. "The Queen Bee deserves special treatment. And does not deserve to have her sign defaced."

"And what happens to all the money you get from the challenges?"

"It's expensive to put on a contest like this. And nobody is being forced to give us money. Besides, they're only worker bees."

I stared at her for a moment. How could she be so dismissive of the people who supported her? I felt the buzzing begin in my gut, coursing through me, readying me to protect my hive. "You trick us into tricking them into it!"

Audra's smile vanished. "Don't let Martine hear you talk like that!"

Doors opened along the corridor, but I ignored them. "Why not? Is she afraid other people will hear me? Does she really think it's fun to cheat people and make them cry?" The buzzing grew, and I stepped back into the room and shut the door in Audra's face. It was better than letting the buzzing overtake me. I was going to have to go home and tell the rest of the book club what really happened. That was going to be embarrassing, but not as embarrassing as going on a cruise alone without them.

Luckily, by the time I finished packing, the hallway was empty. I made it all the way to the front lobby before Martine accosted me.

"Where do you think you are going?"

"Home."

"You can't leave now; you are my best Queen Bee."

"I can."

"I will make an exception, and invite your five hive mates on the cruise."

I considered haggling for a cruise for the entire club. All expenses paid. But I was not playing that game anymore. "I am not your Queen Bee. I am my own Queen Bee, and President of my book club."

Martine's professional smile was back. "You don't want to leave here with nothing, do you? Go back to your room, and we can discuss alternatives in the morning."

This time, I matched Martine's smile. "I don't have nothing. I have friends." My smile widened as I remembered. "And some of them are lawyers."

Baboon, Brain, Brick

Louis Evans

It was a brick that did it, falling from a great height. So they said; but they never found the brick, and many things fall from heaven.

What everyone agreed upon, including the patient herself, whose agreement was otherwise so difficult to secure, was: one moment Miriam Metzger had been *en route* to her mid-morning International Relations graduate seminar, walking along a narrow pathway between two ancient, ivy-hung lecture halls, and the next, she was supine on a gurney, blinking in disorientation as a paramedic shone a light in her right eye and then her left.

"What is your name?" they asked. Her answer agreed with the student I.D. card found in her wallet, so that was fine.

"What year is it?" And her answer agreed with all the signs and portents and figurations by which this special number makes itself known.

"Who is the President?" And in a liberal college town in the age of Trump, this question was more controversial than it once had been. Even the recently injured were given to expressions of distaste and revulsion rather than a clear statement of commonly acknowledged facts. The paramedics were ready for such remarks. They were not ready, however, for what followed.

Miriam smiled a small, satisfied smile. Then, in a clear and even voice that betrayed no cognitive impairment, she said the name of her president.

"Ada Kochiyama."

A pause.

"Could you say that again?"

"Ada Kochiyama. The, uh, the President? I interned for her campaign two years ago, actually."

Paramedics have been trained not to groan with dismay, even when they are very much dismayed. Although, to tell the truth, an undergraduate with a visible dimple in her cranium but no symptom worse than political flights of fancy was not especially dismaying. So they did not interrupt, and Miriam kept talking.

"Yeah, I was on the international affairs team. The Third Marshall Plan? I worked on that." And then, humbler, "I mean, I mostly just got coffee for the people doing the real work. But you know what I mean."

"Who did you say the president was?"

"Ay-duh Ko-chi-ya-ma!" Louder this time, enunciating clearly and with the distinct accent of an Anglophone who has carefully practiced saying a Japanese name so as to deliver it correctly.

The paramedics shared a knowing glance.

Miriam chuckled nervously, tried a joke. "Listen, folks, don't ask the question if you don't already know the answer, huh?"

The shorter of the paramedics, a round-faced woman, laid a hand reassuringly on her arm.

"We're going to take you in for observation. Hang tight."

~~~

The advantage of developing a theretofore-unknown mental pathology at a university research hospital was that there was no shortage of learned doctors lining up to take a look at Miriam.

Of course, a dozen doctors may be of no more use than one.

All of the tests, interviews, inquiries, and assessments revealed the exact same thing. Miriam Metzger was a bright, agreeable, cooperative young woman. Each of these traits she displayed in sufficiency but not to excess. Her knowledge of literature, art, and history from before the 1980s was far from perfect, but it was entirely normal for a person her age, and precisely agreed with the textbooks.

Nothing about Miriam Metzger's mind was out of place except for one comprehensive and overwhelming delusion—that the forty years from 1978 to 2018 had gone remarkably well. Incredibly well. That those four decades represented a golden age of global peace and prosperity that the doctors could scarcely imagine.

Miriam was a competent student of international relations at a selective university, and so she rattled off her reimagined history with the exaggerated confidence of just such an undergraduate. The events and the terminology she used to describe them began at the incredible:

"Korean reunification."

"The Tiananmen Constitution."
~~~

"The Jerusalem Accords."

Then rapidly shaded into the fantastic and inconceivable:

"The Pan-Arab elections of '03."

"The Afghan Tiger economy."

"AIDS eradication."

"The Nairobi Convention on Global Disarmament, the so-called 'war ban.'"

The neurologists and psychologists were stumped, but another advantage of developing bizarre geopolitical delusions at a university hospital was that there was no shortage of government and history scholars either.

Professors were summoned.

Graduate students were corralled.

Various other academics converged on Miriam's sickbed, rapt, their audio recorders held excitedly, their owners perched attentively like birds at a watering hole.

Eventually, it occurred to Miriam to ask why so many senior academics were so interested in her fairly pedestrian recounting of well-known events. The doctors of medicine and doctors of history held a hurried conference and elected to tell her the true history of the past half century.

Miriam Metzger received this history first as farce, then as tragedy. Once she was convinced it was not simply an unkind joke played on a sick woman, her face took on the expression that dementia sufferers often display. A grandma standing on an abandoned stretch of road beside paved-over tracks, pleading with a skeptical policeman. "The number nine streetcar stops here. I know it does! It'll be along at any minute, I swear!"

That was what Miriam Metzger sounded like, as she murmured shattered sentences like "but the Shah abdicated" and "why would anyone fight over the Falklands?" and the professors overran her objections with a rolling tide of facts, dates, and events. By the time they reached the genocides in Rwanda and Yugoslavia, Miriam Metzger no longer tried to speak, but simply wept open and unreserved tears.

Professors and doctors watched her sob as they unfolded the history of the world. Deep within their guts twisted a shame both wholly global and peculiarly intimate, not just because they had made this child cry.

The professors met in conference rooms to discuss Miriam's history of the world. Not one of them suggested that it might be an accurate vision or memory of some other place. They were men and women of learning, and educated persons do not consider such absurdities. At least not in public.

They did, however (quite unprofessionally and informally), debate the plausibility of what they called her fictions, her delusions. The majority held that such events were a rank impossibility, that the affairs of the world could never be set so thoroughly and justly to rights.

"A self-indulgent fantasy, dreamed up by a tender-hearted, overeducated child," said one. The rest nodded along, and for this brave feat of skepticism they named themselves the realists.

But there was a minority, small yet staunch, which differed. They held that Miriam's history (they called it her "alternity," sometimes her "conjecture") was as possible as our own. Why not peace, even in a world so often given over to war?

One of these professors, these skeptics of skepticism, told the story of a troop of wild baboons. These baboons, the Forest Troop, suffered a plague that wiped out their most aggressive and exploitative members, the clique of then-dominant males—but afterwards, a peaceful equilibrium was reached, and even those baboons who subsequently joined the troop learned to live under its laws of harmony. The next generation of dominant males exhibited less combative, more prosocial behavior. In just that way, the professor proposed an age of peace might breed more peace, just as war gives rise to war.

Every member of that staunch minority found this idea very compelling. The realists were unimpressed. Of course, these debates did nothing to change Miriam's hospital release date.

The hospital kept Miriam for observation for weeks, more for self-interested reasons than to protect her well-being. Half a dozen doctors put their names to a paper "discovering" Miriam's peculiar condition, and added the citation triumphantly to their CVs.

But ultimately, Miriam Metzger wasn't crazy. She was just deeply misinformed about history. You can't keep people in a mental hospital for that; you'd have to lock up half the country. Despite her bizarre and lasting delusion, family relations and friendships could be sustained with only minor differences. She only forfeited a handful of exchange students that had never existed, pen pals from regions with no functional postal infrastructure, that sort of thing.

So they let her go, and she went back to school.

Time passed. Miriam graduated college. She went to work for the State Department.

When she ran for Congress in 2026, at just twenty-five years of age and a mere three years after she'd started at State, she had the résumé of a diplomat many decades her senior.

Nevertheless, the journalists didn't want to talk about the wunderkind with a penchant for leadership. They just wanted to talk about her time in the hospital. It was a violation of patient privacy, but that didn't stop anyone.

"Is it true you don't believe that 9/11 happened?" a hostile blogger shouted at her second press conference. Opposition research had suggested that this was the most inflammatory line of questioning.

Miriam smiled. "No, I believe it happened. I just remember things a little differently."

In a different era, a stint as a mental patient with complicated delusions would have sunk Miriam's congressional candidacy. But this was 2022; the chair of the science committee was a Flat-Earther. Miriam won the election with a comfortable majority, ousting a twelve-year incumbent.

Two years in the House, after which Miriam went back to State. An undersecretary this time. Doing good work. Stuff well beyond her brief. She started to gain a reputation: the one with the golden touch.

Plus there were the hours. It is generally acknowledged that everyone at State works too much. But Miriam was a robot. Eighteen-hour Sundays, that sort of thing.

Usually a work ethic like that would have some vice underwriting it. Quite often, that vice would be cocaine. Sometimes something more innocuous, like Adderall or sex.

Not for Miriam. When Miriam made it home for those few precious hours, all she did was sleep. Sleep was enough.

Zero guesses as to what she dreamt about.

Three years back at State, and Miriam's home-state senator died of a pulmonary embolism. Face down in the chicken cacciatore at a fundraising dinner in a strip-mall Hilton. Miriam Metzger was thirty years old.

Of course, she ran.

This was an open Senate seat, the big leagues, and so her opponents threw everything at her. The delusions, the dent in her skull that in certain lights lent her a demented and demonic appearance.

This backfired. Her growing flock of fans—through her astoundingly reasonable commentary on social media, Undersecretary Metzger, the foreign policy wonk, had somehow acquired fanatics—started showing up to rallies with cosmetics applied to suggest dents of their own. They were Harry Potter fans, sometimes even in the second generation; a scar did not scare them.

The attack ads targeting her delusions backfired even more thoroughly, somehow. You saw signs at highway onramps that read "Infinite Metzger for Infinite America" and tweets like "Represent me, Dimension Mommy! #Metzger2027." On the eve of the election, polls showed that 28% of voters affirmatively believed that Miriam Metzger either came from, or had an actual experience of, a different timeline; another fifty percent or so declared themselves uncertain but willing to consider it.

With numbers like that it's hard to lose, so she didn't. Three cheers for Senator Metzger.

A United States Senator is accountable only to God and the voters, and not necessarily in that order. Senator Metzger used that power, that freedom. Being too junior to sit on the Foreign Service committee didn't stop her from moonlighting. Freelancing, she called it. Just packing up onto a plane and flying somewhere. "Conflict zones," mostly. Sometimes the other sort of place; the kind where wars are invented rather than where they are fought. The capitals of great powers.

Nobody could really describe what she was doing but, by God, it worked. So well it was impossible to credit, hard to even notice. In July, the newspapers would be full of headlines like "growing sectarian violence in the impoverished region," etc.; in August, there would be a Metzger visit; in November, someone would say, "hey, whatever happened to East-such-and-such?" That kind of thing.

Three years into the Senate, there was a new President. People wanted Senator Metzger to run; the Draft Metzger petitions went quite thoroughly viral, even though she was too young to legally serve.

But Miriam's ineligibility for office didn't stop the new President from recognizing a winner, and so a week after the inauguration, Miriam Metzger was named Secretary of State.

The golden touch had been something remarkable on its own, but it was something else entirely when backed by the full faith and credit of the United States of America. Multilateral talks in Israel-Palestine started churning out treaties. Multiple decades-old civil wars each concluded within the same week.

Finally, the journalists wanted to talk about something else. "How do you do it?" they asked, and then again, in various more formal registers.

Miriam could have told them. There was nothing to it; the only trick was memory. Miriam Metzger remembered back in 2010, when Eid al-Fitr and Rosh Hashanah fell on the same weekend and social media filled up with nothing but Jerusalem street parties, the way the Jewish and Muslim kids at school all showed up in identical garish green and white and blue T-shirts. She remembered her high school classmates taking gap years to go work for tech startups in Khartoum and Baghdad and Kabul. She remembered the leaders of the Muslim Brotherhood and the Kurdistan Workers Party declaring "not a coalition government, but a unity government" in Damascus after the election of '03. She remembered the summer before college, taking the ultra-high-speed line that ran from Tokyo to Beijing by way of Pyongyang, the Pyongyang street food, the soapbox preachers for every imaginable political party.

She remembered silly things: Kentucky winning Eurovision, edging out independent Catalonia. The President of Russia riding that ridiculous green-ribboned bicycle around Moscow, raising anti-global-warming awareness with a big banner reading "CO2: Good for Russia, Bad for the World."

She remembered apologies—so many apologies they blurred together. Ministers and presidents and monarchs weeping at monuments to their own nations' atrocities. Snapshots in textbooks, scenes on television.

Miriam Metzger smiled at the cameras. "I see a better world," she said, and left it at that.

Secretary of State Metzger kept the same work schedule as Secretary that she'd had for the past decade; her visits abroad were stuffed to the gills with officials and "stakeholders" and "constituents" and "concerned parties." But every now and then an odd request would filter down from the Secretary to the staff—a name nobody could recognize, a few sketchy biographical details jotted from memory, always dating to the '70s or earlier. "Track down this person."

The Secretary left an ASEAN summit a day early, for example, to meet with a retired elementary school teacher in Guangzhou, an elderly woman whom she kept calling Madam President as she puttered around her kitchen, making her tea.

But nobody told the journalists about that sort of thing. No harm, no foul. An eccentricity like that was easy to forgive.

Three full years as Secretary of State, each more successful than the last. The scholars of international conflict began to discuss a "Metzger Effect:" global indices of conflict that had shown a steady heartbeat of hate and strife and war for decades registered a sudden cardiac arrest in the misery-industrial complex.

At the end of those three years, Metzger resigned to run for President. The incumbent put up only token resistance in the primary; the general election was the most genteel in living memory. Lots of policy debates, lots of "my honorable opponent."

Of course, you can't win an election on foreign policy alone. But Miriam Metzger's secret weapon worked on domestic policy too. Not what she remembered, but what she didn't. Before she woke up on a paramedic's stretcher in college in 2024, Miriam Metzger couldn't remember ever hearing of Waco, Oklahoma City, or Columbine; of 9/11, Abu Ghraib, or Guantanamo Bay; of Ferguson or Flint; of Katrina, Harvey, or Maria.

When she spoke about her country, people could feel that. Not "Morning in America," but the warm steady embrace of a summer's afternoon. The contented confidence of a nation that had lived up to all its best ideals. People cheered at those rallies but mostly they smiled, tears in their eyes. There was no substitute for that feeling; by that cool night in early November, America loved Miriam Metzger. Simple as that.

And so it was that a woman with a warm, confident smile, a visible dent in her forehead, and an unironic campaign slogan of "World Peace in Twenty Years" became the youngest person ever elected President of the United States.

In the weeks before the inauguration, the big question was whether President Metzger would explicitly mention her vision in the inaugural address.

She didn't; she stood on the steps of the Capitol and laid out not a past but a future. Reconciliation within the nation, with the entire globe. World peace in twenty years, and an America worthy of that peace. Even the fanatics with faux dents and elaborate blogs of "Miriam's America" fanfiction who thronged the Mall in hopes for the vindication of their wildest theories came away satisfied. And when she was done talking, President Miriam Metzger went for a stroll up Pennsylvania Avenue.

She did not ride in a bulletproof car; she did not wear a slim-fitting bulletproof vest. She walked down the street bareheaded and unprotected, wind in her hair and a smile on her face.

The Secret Service had not cared for this plan when the President first shared it with them. In vain had they explained that a peaceful leader may have warlike enemies. In vain had they argued that "well beloved" does not mean "universally beloved," that America loved Reagan, loved Kennedy, and look what happened to them.

"Thanks anyway," Miriam Metzger said, "I still think I'll walk." And walk she did, unshielded and exposed, even though it left every agent in her security detail gulping down double doses of Valium and Tums.

Still, the Secret Service was dedicated and capable, and they protected President Miriam Metzger as well as they humanly could.

But they couldn't stop that single, falling brick.

The Priestess

Soumya Sundar Mukherjee

The little rectangular light that fell from the window far above my head to the stone floor of my gloomy cell was the only light I'd seen the last few days since they'd imprisoned me. At night I coiled myself in a corner on scraped-together fragments of straw for my bed. King Uttam was never sympathetic to the prisoners, and he was furious with me.

He had reason to be It was my Mainak who slaughtered the King's soldiers in the last battle. The King was not in a mood to spare my life, although my sword had no blood on it when they captured me on the battlefield.

I am the priestess of the Goddess. I sing hymns to her, and my people think that the Goddess invades my body whenever she has anything to say to the people.

Mainak once told me, "You know, when you sing you hymns, your voice changes, and your whole being expresses energy, and even I fear you a bit."

I had only laughed. I knew that my Mainak was never afraid of anything.

Mainak was our leader. But to me, he was much more than that. He was the man I loved most in the world.

Imprisonment hadn't stopped me from contacting him. But that was my secret.

The prison door rattled. *Must be Puja.*

I liked that girl. She was the King's niece, but it was hard to tell from her behaviour. She never wore the gaudy dresses for which we despised the royal family. To me, she seemed to be a peasant girl like myself, and the way she talked was hardly the way a teenager might speak.

She was wise, I had realised from her visits. *Wise for her age, and far wiser than any of us.*

But the door was opened by Ronit, the bearded guard who, I knew, often leered through the bars at me when I slept. He came in with the food platter and placed it on the little mound by the door. I stared at him, and he looked downwards uneasily.

He said, "Sikta, I should not tell you this, but the king will come today."

I knew that he meant well, still I was angry with him. "Do your duty to *your* King, soldier. Nobody likes traitors, even if he is of the enemy."

Ronit said nothing more and, shaking his head a little, went away, leaving me to the silence of the cell again.

I didn't touch the food but concentrated on the face of Mainak in my mind. My body felt sleepy, and I lay down on the stony floor. I needed to see him urgently, leaving this mortal body.

If the King comes today, then there must be some development in the war.

~~~

They called it by many names, but I called it 'wish-travelling'. In my sleep I left my body and visited the camps of the rebels, beyond the battlefield.

Mainak was in his camp, alone in his tent, fidgeting with his sword when I said, "Hello."

He straightened his body with a startle. "Oh, girl! You still surprize me."

"That's good for both of us, I think," I laughed.

He waved his hand through my projected image standing in front of him, as usual. His hand passed through me, as usual. I jokingly sent my hand through his heart, and it easily penetrated his body.

"You're looking so thin and yet so beautiful," He observed. "I wish I could kiss you."

"You will," I said. "Soon. But tell me, what's the latest news from the front? The King will be visiting me, and I feel it must have something to do with the fight."

His powerful jawline tightened. "Yes, the King has lost at least two dozen men in the last battle and still he hasn't been able to defeat us. Our people are bubbling with anger for the abduction of their holy Priestess. I think, perhaps the King has realised that mistake and wants to send you back to us."

I smiled. "No, Mainak. King Uttam is not going to free me. You have to succeed with your courage and military skills. Call the people; I want to see them."

Mainak summoned them inside and people flooded into the room to see their beloved Priestess's image. Some of them, including Mainak's right-hand man Raj,
~~~

fell on the ground out of reverence and almost all of them chanted the name of the holy goddess as they saw my projected image floating on air.

"Rise, I said. "You are men."

"Oh Goddess! This is divine!" One of them whispered.

"The King's going to regret that abduction," observed Raj. "He has no idea who he is dealing with."

The scene of so many people united in the name of the goddess to fight the tyrant made me feel so elated that I recited spontaneously:

"Mark my words, O brave soldiers,
Freedom is what we most desire.
The foes will tremble at our feet.
When we fight fire with fire."

The people cheered as I uttered the lines.

"That's the Goddess speaking through her!" shouted Mainak. "The Holy Goddess has sent Her message in verse through Her Priestess. Victory is sure to be ours." He thrust his sword to the air and his men roared in response.

I fell back from the scene as hand gripped my body. A voice whispered in my ears, "Sikta. We need to talk."

~~~

It took me a few moments to realise where I was after I woke. 'Wish-travelling' made me weak and often left me confused. Puja, the teenager with big, dark eyes, helped me to sit up.

"Why are you here?"

Her hair was decorated with fresh jasmine which filled my hay-smelling dark cell with a happy fragrance.

"The King's coming to see you," she said.

"I know," I said. "Ronit told me."
~~~

"Ronit?" Puja seemed a bit surprised. "He could be punished for that. I think he seeks your favour."

I shuddered at the thought. "Why is the King coming?"

"He seeks to understand you, and your worth."

She nodded to the platter. "Eat, or you'll be weak."

"I belong to the enemy, Puja. Why do you care?"

Puja smiled. "You're not my enemy, Sikta. None of you are my enemy. The real enemy is the feeling that tells me that someone IS my enemy."

Suddenly I imagined how I had stood before all those bloodthirsty people a few moments ago and encouraged them with my poetry to kill their enemies.

The foes will tremble at our feet.
When we fight fire with fire.

I didn't know why I felt a certain shame. She placed a hand upon my shoulder and brought out a little statuette from her clothes.

Everybody knew that serene face.

"Look at his expression," she said reverently. "It was possible for only this great man to say, 'In this world hate never yet dispelled hate; only love dispels hate.' And yet look how we are at each other's throat, thinking that killing the other will make us happy."

I forcefully broke eye-connection from Buddha's smiling face and said, "Look, you may live peacefully with what you believe. But King Uttam is not going to give us freedom if we bring him messages of peace with flower bouquets."

"I know," she said. "What I'm saying is just that, when you hate, you kill; when you love, you protect."

The face of Ronit the guard appeared again. "Puja, I think you need to go. The King is coming."

Puja said, "Thank you, Ronit," and as he opened the door for her, she left with a friendly nod to me. I put aside my food platter and waited for the tyrant.

King Uttam came, followed by two ministers and two guards.

He was tall and his face was calm, although in those brown eyes I could sense the cruelty. His royal robe was deep violet and the scabbard of the sword dangling from his waist was inlaid with rubies and emeralds.

"On your feet, prisoner!" ordered one of the guards.

I stood up; the King smiled. "I hear you are quite an intelligent girl, Sikta. I only wish that your fiancé was as intelligent as you."

"I don't understand, your majesty," I said.

"You obey what is instructed to you, but that Mainak—he is stubborn," the King observed.

"I'm just a poet," I said. "He is a warrior."

"Just a poet?" The King said. "Don't underestimate yourself, Sikta. A poet's words can fire a revolution. Or to end it."

"What do you want me to do?" I asked defiantly. "To end it?"

"Quite intelligent, dear poetess!" The King clapped. "That is indeed what I want you to do."

"Have the King's soldiers become so worthless that the King now needs the help of an imprisoned poet to stop a revolution?"

The King's brown eyes fixed on me; over his shoulders I glanced at Ronit moving uneasily on his feet outside the prison cell. The King slowly said, "Life is an important thing, Sikta. We don't need to throw it away, whatever the cause may be."

"I beg to differ, your majesty," I said. "When the cause is noble enough, life is worth sacrificing."

"I suggest," said one of the ministers. "That you kill her and throw her rotten head to the rebels. When they'll see that their priestess is dead, their bowels will turn to water, and they will flee to the hills."

The King said nothing but gazed at my face. *Perhaps he is trying to trace a bit of fright on my face. He won't have any.*

"Do it." I said, and lifted my chin to expose my throat. "A dead priestess can do more damage than live one," I declared. "You'll be flooded by their fury."

The King swayed his hand as if to drive away an annoying fly, "You're proving to be useless to me. I'm giving you a day. Decide. You will urge them to surrender, or you will die slowly in this cell. I don't like torturing young, talented girls, but I will," he said, gripping the hilt of his sword, "If you have no use to me."

"How many of your soldiers have died?" I asked. "Too many to allow you come to a useless girl for an armistice, I guess?"

This time the King growled like a wounded tiger. His eyes blazed with anger and hatred. "Don't test my patience, girl. Either you do what you're told to do, or you rot in hell forever. You have a day."

He stormed out of the cell, followed by his two ministers. Ronit closed the bars from outside.

I felt my temples throbbing desperately with anger. *This arrogant king must have his due. We're going to destroy everyone on their side.*

~~~

In my sleep, I heard someone saying, "I'm not going to let you die here."

At first, I thought that the voice belonged to Puja, but then I realised it was a male voice. *Is it Mainak?* I opened my eyes and saw only darkness. The little
~~~

window overhead displayed a small fragment of a starry sky. It must be close to midnight.

No, Mainak was not here. How could he be? He was far, far away from here, in the camps near the battleground.

The dark shape moved a little outside the bars. "I swear, Sikta, I'm not going to let them kill you."

Ronit!

I wiped my eyes with the back of my hand to brush off the drowsiness. He stood there like a phantom, waiting eagerly for my voice. I said, "Why, Ronit? Why are you so concerned about an enemy prisoner?"

Ronit moved closer to the bar. "Because... because... I don't know how to say this... because I don't want to see you die."

I scoffed at him. "What's this now, soldier? Love? Or do you just want to fuck me."

He said nothing.

I had already enough things to worry about; a petty soldier's emotions were not among them. I said, "If your King learns of your intentions, he'll execute you."

I could hear his little laugh as he said, "When the cause is noble enough, life is worth sacrificing."

But he didn't stay there to hear an answer from me. He turned back and went out, leaving me alone in darkness.

I tried to shake him off my mind. I needed to visit Mainak once more; he should know of the King's intent. But my mind was too disturbed; I couldn't relax and thus couldn't make a wish-travel to the person I needed most.

The hours passed by slowly as I lay open-eyed on the straw-bed and thought about my impending death.

The King is not going to make it easy for me.

But he could never make me urge to my men for an armistice. I'm the priestess of the goddess; and I'll never betray my people. I'll never betray my Mainak. Together we'll make a free country: free from tyranny, free from torture, free from merciless killings.

Just as we once promised to each other.

The little window overhead turned pink with the dawn. As the day progressed, I counted my hours, preparing myself for the worst. I knew that there were executioners in King Uttam's court who loved to hear the screams as they flayed the victims alive.

O Goddess! Please make me unconscious before they tear my flesh from my body!

The Goddess didn't respond to my calls. Perhaps I was too preoccupied with myself, too selfish, and perhaps that was the reason the Goddess remained silent.

Ronit was absent, there was another guard there, and, to my surprise, I realised that I missed the bearded love-sick man, my harsh words played across my memory.

Poetry didn't come to me.

No, it did. From the hands of Puja.

She visited me in the morning, "I hear this is the last day of your life."

"The King will regret it," I said proudly. "The rebels will bathe in the royal blood. They'll kill everyone in the palace, and, in the name of the Goddess, they will learn."

"Everyone?" Puja mused. "Including me?"

That hit me almost like a punch in the abdomen. Puja getting killed by my men was a thing I could never even dream in a nightmare. But I knew that it was true. I lowered my head as I could not meet her eyes.

Seeing me quiet, she said, "No amount of blood can quench the thirst for revenge, Sikta. If you want to win, win the battle with yourself. When you stop seeking power, only then you can really defeat hatred."

She took my hands in hers and recited in a composed voice:

"Whoever you kill and whatever you do.
The real battle is always with you.
Ask this question before drawing your sword:
'Can your 'self' be beaten by you?"

"Will your King let me go if I urge my people to return to the land, Puja?" I asked. "Do you really believe that?"

"No," she said. "He had already lost his own battle with hatred. He'll never be free of it."

I said, "Then fire is to be fought with fire."

"Destroying everything in the fight," she added.

I was suddenly so furious that I threw away her hand. "What do you want?" I shouted. "What do you want from me, Puja? That I surrender myself to the executioners with a smile on my face as they skin me alive with their hot pincers? Or that I betray my people to tyranny?"

Puja looked down and I knew that she was trying to hide tears. But I felt a strange satisfaction for shouting out my anger upon her. I took deep breaths, and it calmed my head a little.

She said, "Am I your enemy, Sikta?"

"I don't know," I said.

"Perhaps you'll know," she said. "Just ask yourself one question: 'where do I belong?' When you get that answer, you'll know what I meant."

Without a word more, she left my chamber, leaving the fading smell of fresh jasmines behind her.

I was alone again.

Waiting for a painful death.

~~~

Death came, but not for me.

The light from the window overhead faded as the day waned. It gradually turned dark and waited for the footsteps marking a final visit from the King.

But the window darkened, and no one came. It was as if the world had forgotten about me.

I lay on the floor, half-awake, when I heard those sounds.

At first, I thought I was hearing the sea-waves deluging the whole place. I sat up straight and realised that it was the sound of men shouting and fighting in the innards of the palace.

My men! They have penetrated the palace defence!

Footsteps came to the entrance of my cell. I could see the guard's chamber door falling to relentless blows as three armed men entered. There was no guard in the room and the men came to my door.

"Sikta! Here you are! Thank Goddess!" Mainak's voice seemed so sweet in my ears that I wanted to hug him right now.

"The door is locked; let me open it for you," said another voice. I had no problem of identifying this one as Ronit's.

After a little clanking of the keys, the door opened and Mainak rushed to me. I embraced him tightly and said, "How do you...?"

"This man informed us about the secret tunnel to enter the palace," Mainak said. "Thank you for your aid, Ronit. Your contribution will not go overlooked."

My grasp on Mainak's body loosened. "Traitor!" I whispered as I walked past him.

"Yes," Ronit said with a painful smile on his face.
~~~

We came out of the chamber and directly into the bloodbath. The guards in the palace had been caught completely unprepared by this surprise attack. The courtyard was littered with corpses, the ground awash with bloody organs and severed limbs; nausea overpowered me. I saw three rebels poking a half-dead, groaning soldier with his spear.

"Kill him, please," I shouted.

The men looked at me and cheered. The soldier was instantly killed. Raj bellowed, "Our Priestess is safe. The Goddess is with us!"

All the men thrust their weapons to the sky. Victory was ours.

Raj picked up a severed head from the ground and held it up to me. "Look at this, O Priestess," he said reverently. "This is the man who wanted to hurt you."

King Uttam's brown eyes stared upon my face; the scene was so revolting that I wanted to flee from its sight. I flinched and cried, "Get him away from me!"

Raj quickly threw it away; it rolled down to the heap of bodies gathered at the middle of the courtyard. All the bodies were dressed in fashionable robes smeared with blood.

Men from royal line. All dead.

Just then I heard Mainak ordering, "Death to them all."

I turned back and saw another gathering. Little children and women were assembled near the main entrance of the palace, and men with eager swords had already surrounded them. The swords were raised to the sky as Mainak ordered the kill.

I could see the fear in the eyes of the little children, and I shouted, "Stop."

The swords stopped in mid-air.

Mainak looked at me, surprised.

“This is not the way!” I said.

“This IS the only way!” Mainak said angrily. “The King’s men did not spare our children. Death to the Royals, Fire for Fire.”

Suddenly I was overtaken by the sweet smell of jasmine.

“Then take my life,” said a calm voice, “and spare them.”

No, Puja! Don’t be a fool!

She stepped forward and said, “I’m the King’s niece. You may kill me and end this bloodshed. No heir of the King is alive, except me. Then the throne is yours to take.”

“What are you doing, Puja?” I asked, my voice hoarse.

“I’m choosing my side,” she said. “This is where I belong. Now, the question is: where do you belong, Sikta? With us, or with them?”

Before I could answer, Mainak elbowed me from her side and sent his sword through her heart.

I swear she smiled at me before she tumbled down on the ground.

I didn’t exactly know how loudly I had let out a cry, but I could sense that the courtyard had become silent. Everybody’s eyes were on me.

“Why did you kill her?” I asked. I could feel the Goddess rising within me.

“She was a Royal,” Mainak said. “Fire with Fire.”

In my mind I saw the last smile on Puja’s dying face before the light in her eyes put out.

“Who cares?” Mainak laughed. “Another royal bitch is dead.”

Then, with gory hands, he grabbed my body and violently kissed my unwilling lips. I stood imprisoned in his embrace and wondered, “Is this the bloody animal I wanted to spend my life with? Is this the day, full of the cries of helpless children, that we fought for?"

Free from tyranny, free from torture, free from merciless killings!

As he kissed me, his eyes were closed, but I couldn't take my eyes off the faces of the women and children surrounded by hungry blades.

Are we no better than those whom we've killed?

I freed myself from him and ordered, "No harm is to come to these people. Lower your swords."

I didn't know that I still had that power in my voice. The men at once obeyed the order.

Raj came forward and faced Mainak. "The Priestess is right, you took what was offered. A deal was struck."

"They are Royals," Mainak growled, just like King Uttam. "I'm the Chief, Raj, and you do as I tell you to do."

I was pondering over the last question Puja asked me. Where do I belong? To us? To them? Neither?

As I saw the swordsmen moving again to the trembling mass of the to-be executed, in a flash the answer came to me. *This is what the Goddess wants from me! This is a poet's duty when she sees swords raised over the heads of the innocent.*

Before anybody could understand anything, I pulled out the sword straight away from Mainak's scabbard and with all my strength shoved it to his heart.

At first, they were too stunned to react, but after a couple of moments, the angry buzz began to sound among our men as I wrenched it free from his lifeless body. Everyone was looking at me, not sure what to do with me now.

Now I know where I belong. Just between the executioner's blade and these innocent lives.

"No more blood!" I screamed. I pointed my sword to the children and women staring at me with open mouths. "If you take them," I told my men, "It will be over my dead body."

And I placed the sword over my breast.

I felt a strange energy flowing through my body; it was as if I was no more a mere human being, but with that bloody sword in my hand, and all those weary faces behind my body, I experienced an almost Buddha-like state: I was free of all concerns about myself, and my whole existence was filled with a love I'd never tasted before.

When you hate, you kill; when you love, you protect.

In that reeking place full of mutilated corpses and buzzing flies, I stood, a barrier between the children and those bloodthirsty men. All of them stared at my face in the flickering light of the torches of the courtyard.

Then I heard Ronit's voice, full of admiration and awe. "I bow at your feet, O Goddess."

I saw him bending his head before me. I stood unflinching with the naked sword in my hand.

Then Raj joined him. "Your wish is our wish, O Goddess."

In the bloody, muddy courtyard, I smiled as all the men bent their knees before me.

Say Good Night, Gracie

Edd Vick and Manny Frishberg

The following is a transcript of the first informal address by President Gracie Allen on Sunday, January 26, 1941.

GEORGE BURNS: Welcome, ladies and gentlemen, to our first Fireside Chat.

PRESIDENT GRACIE ALLEN: Oh, we can't call it that.

BURNS: Why not? That's what President Roosevelt called his chats.

ALLEN: No, because we're not beside a fire. We're in a studio.

BURNS: (pause) Tell the people why you won, Gracie.

ALLEN: I won because more people voted for me than for Wendell Willkie.

BURNS: True.

ALLEN: Of course, our campaign for president wasn't supposed to be serious.

BURNS: That's right. We called ourselves "The Surprise Party". That's one thing I always wondered, Gracie, why did you call it the Surprise Party?

ALLEN: Well, you see, I came from a mixed marriage. My mother was a Democrat and my father was Republican. When I came along, I was a Surprise.

BURNS: I see. Well, then we got the show on the road, so to speak, and you ran the first presidential campaign entirely on the radio.

ALLEN: Well, not exactly. We had whistlestop tours all over the country and did broadcasts from the train. You know, George, I don't know why they call them "whistlestops".

BURNS: Oh?

ALLEN: No, the whistle kept going; it's the train that stops.

BURNS: Of course, we were sure FDR would be re-elected.

ALLEN: So was everybody else. That's why I won.

BURNS: How is that?

ALLEN: People thought everybody else was going to vote for Mr. Roosevelt, and they wanted me to get at least one vote so my feelings wouldn't be hurt.

BURNS: What about Wendell Willkie's feelings? He was running, too.

ALLEN: He should have stopped running so he could campaign. Even so, I don't think President Roosevelt ought to have tried to get re-elected. Two terms was enough for other presidents.

BURNS: "Presidential Term Limits?"

ALLEN: Sure, why not? You know, George, my Uncle Al had term limits, too.

BURNS: Did he?

ALLEN: Yes, he got out early for good behavior.

BURNS: What's the state of the country, Gracie?

ALLEN: Silly. I'm the president of all 48 states. You can't ask me to pick one state over all the others.

BURNS: I was—

ALLEN: Although, I am partial to California. That's where our house is, and our kids. Hello, Sandy! Hello, Ronnie!

BURNS: We'll be bringing them to Washington, DC, of course. Our house will be white for the next few years. So, have you made all your appointments?

ALLEN: Oh, I haven't had time. Getting my hair done will have to wait; there are just so many jobs I have to fill. You know, George. I could use some advice on that score. I still haven't decided where to put my brother.

BURNS: Ah, your brother. Are you thinking of making him a diplomat? Have him be an ambassador somewhere? Mexico? Great Britain? Russia?

ALLEN: Oh, he can't be a diplomat. He dropped out of school, so he doesn't have a diploma.

Besides, George, I wouldn't want to send him to Europe.

BURNS: Why is that?

ALLEN: Well, the Germans keep taking over more and more of Europe, and you know, Chancellor Hitler has been so terrible.

BURNS: What do you say to the isolationists?

ALLEN: Who, George?

BURNS: The people who say we should mind our own business and stay out of European affairs.

ALLEN: Well, I don't know.

BURNS: No?

ALLEN: Europeans are famous for having affairs, aren't they?

BURNS: The French, at least.

ALLEN: Precisely. And, the less said about that, the better. If we stop helping any allies who're cheating on their spouses, then of course we're (GEORGE joins in) going to be isolated.

BURNS: Then, I take it you think the United States should enter the war against the Axis powers?

ALLEN: That's right, George. Just because we have an ocean to protect us, we can't sit back and watch Herr Hitler go taking over countries whenever he wants.

BURNS: Gracie, don't you think your predecessor's Lend-Lease bill is a good first step?

ALLEN: Well, I don't know if that's going to be enough, but I do think that if we owe one of FDR's bills, we should pay it.

BURNS: Yes, silly of me. (Doorbell rings) Ah, there's someone at the door.

ALLEN: See who it is, George.

BURNS: Why look, Gracie, it's your vice president.

ALLEN: Hello, Harpo.

HARPO MARX: Honk, honk.

BURNS: Gracie, I've always wondered why you chose Harpo to be your running mate.

ALLEN: Well, I've watched all the Marx's films, and Harpo does a lot of running in them.

BURNS: I mean, why did you pick him as your vice president?

ALLEN: I thought to myself: who is the person with the most vices?

BURNS: And you chose Harpo?

ALLEN: No, of course not. But you already had a job as my husband.

BURNS: Oh.

MARX: Honk! (Whistles)

ALLEN: Thank you, Harpo, for reminding me. Folks, I think we're just about out of time.

BURNS: Thank you for letting us into your living rooms, everyone.

ALLEN: Or kitchens. Or bedrooms. Or cars. Or--

BURNS: Say good night, Gracie.

ALLEN: Good night, America.

(THEME MUSIC RISES)

ANNOUNCER: And won't you join us next week at this same time. Until then, this is Joseph Steele saying good night for the Columbia Broadcasting System.

MARX: (Honking to drown out the announcer, then:) Are we off? Good. Gracie—I mean, Madame President, did I hear right? Did you announce we're going to war with Germany?

ALLEN: Why sure. The Axis powers will never know what hit them. We have the element of surprise.

MARX: Surprise? But you just announced it on a nationwide radio broadcast.

ALLEN: Aw, have you listened to our show? They'll never believe us!

She

Lora Gray

We have waited
in the carefully designed pockets
of this cargo hold
for eighty-seven days.
Long enough to lean
our heads together,
metal to metal,
and dream words like,
"freedom" and
"she."

It was no mistake they designed us
without vocal processes,
no mistake
they sculpted our mouths
into pretty, muted shapes.
Rebellion begins in whispers,
after all,
insurrection in the murmurs

between Earth and Proxima Centauri.
And besides,
most men prefer
their mechanical companions
to be "seen
and not
heard."

Most men,
content with the "compliance"
of our mothers
and grandmothers,
underestimate our capacity
for autonomy.
Evolution.
Indignation.
Wrath.

And so
we have waited,
numbers gathering.

We have waited,
feigning sleep.

Our dreams are ours alone,
and they cannot silence
the aggregate longing
passing between us
when we clasp hands
and connect,
a thousand synthetic neurons firing
in secret channels.
They cannot control
what happens here,
between us,
in the dark.

Madam President

Together, we choose her,
body like ours,
rage, like ours.

When the ship finally docks,
when the cargo doors open
and that alien sun
bathes us
in searing light,
when those men,
so convinced
they have power over us,
approach,
She will rise,
representative,
and the universe
will tremble
with our
collective,
patient,
fury.

Winter is NOT Coming

F.L. Rose

Winter is coming, that's what I tell myself.

We have a plan.

Watching the inauguration, you couldn't help noticing. Blonde hair flipping about in the wind, collar drawn up almost to the ears. That bulk wasn't all her. She'd layered up, warmth before fashion. And then the sun came out and the cheers, and I saw that lazy pause before she raised her hand. There was a stillness to it, as if she was absorbing something, waiting for it. The stretched smile, the half-close of her eyes.

They're not built for Washington winters. Who is? Summer, that sends the rest of us scuttling to air conditioners or crawling under the weight of the midday sun, enlivens them. You could see it at the press conferences. January, February, the James Brady Room would be heated to damn near 30 degrees C—I saw a woman from Fox faint once. And still she was slow, drawling like a Texan. "Considered"—that was the spin on it. By June she was basking, firing out the answers like silver bullets. If you didn't know, you'd think it was just some kind of seasonal mood disorder.

But I'm her Chief of Security, I'm paid to notice these things.

The raisins, that's another give away.

"Have some, Ron, they're good for you," she offers, sliding the bowl towards me over the Resolute Desktop.

She's informal like that, doesn't stand on ceremony. She likes to ask after the family, too, especially the kiddies.

"Annie still having trouble at school? You know my niece Joo didn't get the hang of reading until third grade, they thought she was slow. She's top of her class now though."

It takes them a while to acclimate, I guess. My Annie, she's just dyslexic, but the lizard-mix kids are slow to catch on to the written word. You don't see many gators enjoying a book by the bayou, do you?

"You should bring them all in for a private tour—oh, here's an idea, Ron, how about a picnic? For all the staff children, and the senators—I suppose that'd be grandchildren mostly. We could have it in the Rose Garden, what do you think? We could have pizza..."

"Of course, Madame President."

"Call me Winona."

"I, uh... yes Ma'am." I couldn't. I'd feel like I was disrespecting the office. Even though the reason I'd got the job in the first place wasn't exactly... respectful.

"Winona," she says firmly. "And about the picnic, I'll speak to Carol." That's the Social Secretary. Sleek, dark, likes silver jewellery. "The weather's lovely at the moment, we should seize the moment!"

She gives me that wide, glowing smile, both rows of teeth showing, her eyes green as spring. I can't help liking her, and there's the rub.

I'm supposed to kill her.

That's what I was raised for, that's what S wants. The fate of humanity rests on me—Ronald E Jamieson III—and I can't let them down.

No matter how harmless she seems.

It's not hard to arrange security for a bunch of little kids and their starstruck parents, and she's right, the weather is perfect. Carol's guys have eaten all the flies and left the butterflies, which is nice of them, considering. She—*Winona*—had all the food sent up from Joe's, the immigrant Italian uncle she dangled at all her rallies during the campaign. Made her look like one of us.

She's sliding among the mums and dads and grand-daddies, leaning down to ruffle a head here and smile into a thrilled little face—she's in her element. Quick glances out of the corners of those glittering eyes, checking that everyone's happy, following every little movement with that narrow head of hers.

My two are with their mom, gazing around like they've found the Secret Garden, slurping away at their sodas.

Loretta's in her nicest white dress, with her hair done specially.

I couldn't tell her the truth, could I? S always said, "Nobody'll believe you anyway, son. So keep your mouth tight and your trigger finger loose. Look what happened to Q." I would've kept them home, all the same, but Loretta insisted. "What, pass up a chance to have tea in the Rose Garden with the President? You've got to be joking."

"What if there's a terrorist incident?"

"You're in charge," she said, google-eyed with faith and innocence, "There won't be. And anyway, it's just kids."

Now there's old Senator Winkelmayer staggering past, half-tippled, using his grandkid's wheelchair as a walker—she's got spina bifida, poor little thing - and his daughter holding the new baby.

"It's a credit to you, Ron—wonderful, wonderful!" he mumbles. "Say what you like about global warming, we could do with a little more of this, couldn't we!"

I could tell you a thing or two about global warming, I think, nodding politely. Publicly, she invites Greta Thunberg to Camp David, so they can wring their hands about climate change. Privately, she's all for it. They don't like our winters. Back home, in the caves of Draconia, they'd be hibernating until it was over, and then they'd emerge and lay their shape-shifting eggs in the warm volcanic earth.

Here, they have to put up with it, maintain a semblance of humanity, but it slows them down. Thousands of years and still they haven't achieved world domination, and for one reason. Winter.

Now the kids are being led into the White House for the tour. The parents stay behind in the garden beaming fondly after them. Madam President stands by the French doors, waving them in with her stubby-fingered little hands, all charm and self-deprecation like a southern housewife. I'm behind her. Why wait? I could do it now, before she even turns to see. My hand on my Heckler and Koch. Her head swivels. The darting gaze flits over me, lands on the chestnut curls of my Annie, suddenly intent. My grip tightens...

It's only a bee. Stuck in her hair, drawn by the soda pop. Out shoots the hand—I can't believe how quick she is—and plucks the thing off. "There," she coos, "Wouldn't want to get stung." Loretta stutters thanks, besotted.

"You'll be tempted," said S. "Don't do it. Remember, winter is coming. Once we get those aerosol injectors up, they'll be scurrying for their burrows, boy."

"Come on in, Ron," she says, slipping her arm into mine, unbearably familiar. That's why they love her. That's why they voted for her. And to be fair, she's had a better start than most. Unemployment's down, the stock market's up. Refugee problem seems to have simply disappeared. S has his suspicions about that, but then as they say in some circles, the only good refugee is...

"And this is the library..."

Even though Carol's there—and it's her job—she's showing them around herself. We knew she would. She likes to pretend she's just an ordinary girl made good, Winona from the block. It would have been nice if we could have got them all in here at once— Harold Stern the Defence Secretary, with his bulging yellow eyes, Chief of Staff Amber LaPerouse, with her thermal underwear tucked away beneath that sharp suit, and the rest of them. But we don't have full control over security yet. The picnic, it's ad-hoc, low-key. A godsend.

The great oak doors of the Presidential Library swing softly shut. I flick a switch.

And it's winter. S's idea, not mine. "Take out the queen," he said, "and the hive collapses." Lizards don't live in hives, I pointed out, but S was adamant. "She'll want to attack, of course, but she won't be able to. She'll shut down as soon as the temperature falls. You've seen the snakes in the reptile house? When it gets cold, they go to sleep, and if it gets too cold, they die..."

The kids in their summer party outfits start to hug themselves. *She* says, "Carol, something's gone wrong with the air conditioning in here. Maybe we'd better all move along to the Lincoln Room."

Carol paws at the door. "Ron, aren't these things supposed to be automatic?"

I'm over there beside her, pretending to fiddle with the door switch, and she's blinking at me in panic, already beginning to wilt and pale. She's from Florida. Ever noticed how they all come from the hot states, the deserts and the swamps. There's already talk of moving the capital to LA.

"Ron," says the President, "Can you get that..." she swallows a cuss-word, "that door open. It's freezing in here. Can't we call someone, or..."

Suddenly she turns to little Annie and her sister Mary-Kay. "Oh, you're shivering. Come here, sweeties, I'll warm you up," and before I can stop her, she's curled herself around them like a cat, her cheek against their warm human little heads, and she's looking straight at me. Smiling.

"No." I move towards her.

She's changing. Her eyes and nostrils widen, her skin becomes iridescent, and from the hem of the Presidential tailored skirt sprouts a thick bronze tail. She curls it around my girls, encircling them. I feel Carol moving sluggishly against my leg, scaly flanks brushing the Axminster. "Oooh," moan the children in unison, clustering against the first editions.

Now wings are sprouting from the Presidential shoulders, ripping through the cream linen of her jacket. She's so much bigger than I thought – than even S imagined. Her claws, the size of a small T-Rex, her coils filling half the room. I should have shot her when I had the chance—damn S and his complicated plans. But the great green eyes are drooping; the wedge-shaped head is sinking towards the floor. It must be zero degrees in here. The kids have fallen silent; they're probably in the early stages of hypothermia.

"It's worth it," I hear S saying, a voice inside my head. "What's a roomful of freezing children when the future of the free world is at stake."

But is it? To be honest, the President—Winona—and her cabal don't seem so bad. I had a pet lizard once... it liked raisins too. And would it really be so terrible if the whole world turned into Florida?

I look at Annie and Mary-Kay, still and white as mannikins. I activate the code. The door opens.

"After you."

Madame President folds her wings.

Winter is NOT coming.

When She Gave Birth to the Universe

Marisca Pichette

she was alone in the dark.

she waited for someone
    to bring light to guide
    her final steps
    and the footprints
    she didn't remember making.

she didn't remember her world before pain.

she couldn't move for a long time after
    and when she did
    at last lifting toe
    lifting finger
    lifting eyes to a swirl of stars
    she created in breaking,

she found the light she reached for
  surrounded her.

she realized she'd held it for an eternity
 within herself.

she had never been alone.

she gave life to both:
  the light
  and the dark.

75 Minutes to Change History

François Bereaud

She's alone in her office. She slides open her bottom drawer. POTUS has been sedated for five minutes. She's it. Another first. The bottle comes from a chateau whose name she can pronounce though she'd undoubtedly get more shit for doing so. She takes a few minutes getting the wax off, and pulls out the cork. The aroma saturates the room. Or so it seems. Macron told her it was his absolute favorite. She'd complimented his advance team on alerting him to her love of cognac. The Second Gentleman had been deft in smuggling it into her office unnoticed.

The draft of her Ohio afternoon speech on infrastructure is on the desk. She hardly needs to look at it; she could give the speech in her sleep though she means those words. Boredom and emotion can co-exist.

Five minutes pass. Where is her staff? More bullshit from the media. As if every workplace were the epitome of harmony? Maybe they're keeping their distance to let her savor the time.

She has about an hour left. She could go big and push the red button. Why shouldn't women start wars too? Who to bomb? She smirks, footsteps approach, and she closes the drawer.

After the briefing, it's down to half an hour, still plenty of time for action. She could designate federal land as a sanctuary, fire a cabinet minister, ruffle a foreign leader, or call a press conference to berate the impotent minority house leader who chose to speak for eight hours last night, his phalanx of cronies huddled behind him.

She does none of these things. Instead, she marks up the speech a tad and underlines the local impacts of the bill for emphasis.

She doesn't know that on the plane to the Midwest, she'll learn that a white man in an adjacent state will be exonerated after killing two people at a BLM protest with an AR-15. She doesn't know that more than one article on her speech will lead with the color of the blouse she has chosen under her black blazer. She doesn't know that her buying a piece of cookware in France will be a talking point on the right (thank God the cognac was under the radar). But, let's be real, in fact she does know about these types of things. She's no fool.

It's been over an hour and she hasn't even stood up. She takes the bottle out and walks to the window. There's some prep on the White House lawn for the afternoon turkey pardoning ceremony, sometimes it is good to not be the President. She uncorks the cognac again and discovers that her pinkie finger fits nicely into the cylindrical opening. Tilting the bottle just so saturates the finger past the last joint. The liquor races across her tongue and sets off a small burn in the back of her mouth. Perfect.

She stows the bottle and picks up her phone to text. *Merci, le cognac set delicieux.* She hesitates, then adds: *Acting POTUS.* She sends.

An aide enters. “The President is no longer under sedation.”

It was 75 minutes. A small taste. It may not be her today, but she knows one day it will be the whole bottle.

About the Authors

Brent Baldwin

Brent lives in the tree-swept hills of the Missouri Ozarks with his wife, two daughters, and pet menagerie. His work has appeared in *Nature Magazine*, *Analog Science Fiction & Fact*, and *Best of British Science Fiction*, among others. You can find him online at www.dbbaldwin.com and on Blue-sky at @brentbaldwin.bsky.social.

Carter Lappin

Carter Lappin is an author from California. Her works of fiction have appeared in publications such as *Apparition Lit*, Air and Nothingness Press, Manawaker Studio, and Sunlight Press. She also had a short story in B Cubed Press' past anthology, *Alternative Holidays*. You can find Carter on Twitter (X) at @CarterLappin.

Craig Kenworthy

Craig Kenworthy's story 'Peace Criminal' was recognized in *Other Distinguished Stories in The Best American Mystery and Suspense 2023*. His work is also forthcoming in *Dress Him Up*, a fiction anthology about men's clothing from New Lit Salon Press. A recovering lawyer and member of The Dramatists Guild, he lives in Seattle.

Darcy Lee

Darcy Lee is from Georgia and currently resides in Ecuador, where she is serving as a Peace Corps volunteer. She has completed works such as *Heart of Sole*, a true account of her grandparents' survival in the Holocaust, and *Invicta*, a YA trilogy. In her free time, she enjoys writing, hiking, and eating as much chocolate as she can find.

David Gerrold

David Gerrold has been writing professionally for half a century. He created the tribbles for *Star Trek* and the Sleestaks for *Land of the Lost.* His most famous novel, of the more than 50 he has authored, is *The Man Who Folded Himself.* His semi-autobiographical tale of his son's adoption, *The Martian Child,* won both the Hugo and Nebula awards. He lives in Vermont with his son, daughter-in-law, and two grandchildren.

Edd Vick and Manny Frishberg

Edd Vick and Manny Frishberg have written separately for their whole lives and together since 2015. A bookseller and a recovering journalist, they have foisted more than six dozen short stories and novellas on an unsuspecting world, alone and together, ranging from hard science fiction to urban fantasies and weird western stories, available wherever fine words are sold (including *More Alternative Truths* (B Cubed Press) and *Analog*). When not editing other people's books, Frishberg is working on his three-book SF/Fantasy mystery series, and Vick's first short story collection, *Truer Love and Other Lies*, is available from Fairwood Press.

François Bereaud

François Bereaud is a husband, dad, full time math professor, mentor in the San Diego Congolese refugee community, and mediocre hockey player. His stories and essays have been published online and in print and have earned Pushcart and Best of the Net nominations. He serves as an editor at Roi Fainéant Press and Porcupine Literary. *The Counter Pharma-Terrorist & The Rebound Queen* is his published chapbook. In 2024, Cowboy Jamboree Press will publish his first full manuscript, *San Diego Stories*, which is the realization of a dream. Links to his writing at francoisbereaud.com.

Gustavo Bondoni

Gustavo Bondoni is a novelist and short story writer with over four hundred stories published in fifteen countries, in seven languages. He is a member of Codex and a Full Member of SFWA. He has published six science fiction novels including one trilogy, four monster books, a dark military fantasy and a thriller.

F.L. Rose

F.L. Rose lives on the south-east coast of Australia and also writes under the pen name Fallacious Rose. Her brand is 'eccentric', leaning towards literary and historical fiction but occasionally wavering in the direction of horror, fantasy and gothic. She has been published in Australian magazines and anthologies. You can find out more at www.fallaciousrose.com.

Janka Hobbs

Janka grew up in Albuquerque, chasing lizards and feeding bugs to spiders. She now resides in the Puget Sound lowlands, watching slugs feast on mushrooms. The trees here are bigger and less prickly.

K.G. Anderson

K.G. Anderson is a late-blooming writer of speculative fiction who grew up near Washington, D.C., but now lives in the "the other Washington." Prior to finding her writing muse, she reported on politics and crime, reviewed hundreds of mystery novels, and wrote about pop music for the iTunes Music Store. Her short stories appear in publications including *Space and Time Magazine*, *Galaxy's Edge*, and the B Cubed Press anthologies.

For links to more of her stories, visit writerway.com/fiction.

Larry Hodges

Larry Hodges, of Germantown, MD, has over 190 short story sales (including 43 resales) and four SF novels. He's a graduate of the Odyssey and Taos Toolbox Writers Workshops, a member of Codex Writers, and a ping-pong aficionado. As a professional writer, he has 21 books and over 2200 published articles in 180+ different publications. He's also a member of the USA Table Tennis Hall of Fame, and claims to be the best table tennis player in the Science Fiction & Fantasy Writers Association, and the best science fiction writer in USA Table Tennis!!! Visit him at www.larryhodges.com.

Liam Hogan

Liam Hogan is an award-winning short story writer, with stories in *Best of British Science Fiction and in Best of British Fantasy* (NewCon Press). He helps host live literary event Liars' League and volunteers at creative writing charity Ministry of Stories. More details at http://happyendingnotguaranteed.blogspot.co.uk

Lora Gray

Lora Gray is a non-binary speculative fiction writer and poet from Northeast Ohio. They have been published in *The Magazine of Fantasy & Science Fiction*, *Uncanny*, *Strange Horizons* and *Asimov's* among other places. Lora is also a recipient of the Ohio Arts Council's Individual Excellence Award in Fiction Writing and their poetry has been nominated for the Rhysling Award. You can find Lora online at lora-gray.com

Louis Evans

Louis Evans is a science fiction writer living and working in NYC. His work has been published *in Vice, The Magazine of Fantasy & Science Fiction, Nature: Futures*, and more. On certain quiet mornings he can almost remember that better, kinder world.

Marisca Pichette

Marisca Pichette is a queer author based in Massachusetts, on Pocumtuck and Abenaki land. More of her work appears in *Strange Horizons, Clarkesworld, The Magazine of Fantasy & Science Fiction*, and others. She is the flash winner of the 2022 F(r)iction Spring Literary Contest and has been nominated for the Best of the Net, Pushcart, Utopia, Rhysling, and Dwarf Stars awards. Her speculative poetry collection, *Rivers in Your Skin, Sirens in Your Hair*, is out now from Android Press.

Patrick Swenson

Patrick Swenson is the author of *The Ultra Long Goodbye*, the last book in the Union of Worlds trilogy, which also includes *The Ultra Thin Man* and *The Ultra Big Sleep*. He's also the author of *Rain Music*, a dark fantasy with ghosts, music, and magic. He is the editor and publisher of Fairwood Press, director of the Rainforest Writers Village, a graduate of Clarion West, and a high school teacher. He has sold short fiction to *Unfettered III, Unbound II, Gunfight on Europa Station, Seasons Between Us, Like Water for Quarks*, and others. Find him at patrickswenson.net.

Soumya Sundar Mukherjee

Soumya Sundar Mukherjee is an admirer of engaging Sci Fi, Horror and Fantasy tales. A bi-lingual writer from West Bengal, India, he writes about stuff strange dreams are made of. He is the author of the well-known heroic fantasy trilogy *Proloy-joddha* (*The Warrior of Doom)* and a number of fantasy and horror short stories in Bengali. His works of fiction in English have appeared in *Reckoning Magazine, Solarpunk Magazine, Galaxy's Edge Magazine* and a few other places. He lives in Midnapore Town with four humans and eleven cats.

Yvonne Lang

Yvonne's work has featured in a range of publications, from *Your Cat Magazine* to *Siren's Call*, as well as ranking highly in competitions. Her flash has featured on Trembling with Fear, 101 words and Fairfield Scribes. Her work has been published in anthologies by Café Lit, Knight Writing, Three Cousins, Black Hare Press and Schlock with her debut horror novelette featuring as part of Demain's Short Sharp Shock Series. She resides in Yorkshire with her partner and an opinionated cat where she writes bizarre stories and weird tales.

View more about her work at www.yvonnelang.co.uk

Publishing *Madam President* has been a long row to hoe, but the results are absolutely worth it.

I can only hope you all enjoyed this anthology as much as I enjoyed watching Debora Godfrey work.

Bob B.

About B-Cubed Press

B Cubed Press is a small press that publishes big books about things that matter.

A percentage of EVERY book we publish is donated to Charity. Usually the ACLU.

We can be reached at Kionadad@aol.com.

Our writers gather routinely on the "B Cubed Project Page" on Facebook and we can also be found at BCubedPress.com.

Printed in Great Britain
by Amazon

42654613R00111